" ... . "

Matt eyed his horse dubiously.

"Horses are usually pretty good judges of character,"
Jamie commented.

Matt shot her a look. "You know what you need?"

For a moment she seemed taken aback. "I have a
feeling you're not talking about money in the bank
or good health."

"What you need more than anything right now is
some great sex."

Her eyes widened, but she retained her composure.
"And I suppose you know someone who could provide
that."

"I've put smiles on a few women's faces in my time."

"You're incredible ... and I don't mean that as a
compliment. I've heard there were men in this world
like you," she said, swinging up onto her horse. "But
until yesterday I'd been lucky enough not to meet any."

Matt's horse snorted and glared at him with
unfriendly eyes.

That did it. He had to put up with a frustrated
woman whose sharp tongue and knockout body
drove him crazy, and now he was stuck with the
horse from hell.

ABOUT THE AUTHOR

Kathy Clark wanted to be a cowboy when she grew up and was devastated to discover the Old West was dead. Combining her love for horses, the Rocky Mountains and cowboys in tight jeans, she has written a story set in the New West.

Kathy lives in Colorado with her husband and their three sons.

Books by Kathy Clark

HARLEQUIN AMERICAN ROMANCE

KATHY CLARK

GOODBYE, DESPERADO

Harlequin Books

TORONTO • NEW YORK • LONDON
AMSTERDAM • PARIS • SYDNEY • HAMBURG
STOCKHOLM • ATHENS • TOKYO • MILAN
MADRID • WARSAW • BUDAPEST • AUCKLAND

Published April 1993

ISBN 0-373-16481-5

GOODBYE, DESPERADO

Chapter One

Slowly the sun sank behind the jagged peaks of the Rocky Mountains.

Matt studied the sentence on the computer screen. How many times in the past ten years had he written those same words in that same way? Surely there was a fresh way to describe a sunset. His finger pressed on the backspace key and deleted the line.

The flaming scarlet sun melted into the rugged horizon, splashing molten red stains on the lofty, snow-capped mountain peaks.

He shook his head. No, too many adjectives. After all, this was just a sunset. If he wasn't careful, his descriptions of the landscape would have more personality than his characters. And Duke King, the hero of his novels, wouldn't appreciate being upstaged by Mother Nature.

Once again the cursor backed up until it left the screen empty.

As night approached, the sun fled...

Matt read the words aloud, then deleted them at the mental image of the sun sprouting legs and jogging across the horizon.

*The darkness crept across the sky, pushing the sun
behind the rugged mountain peaks that stretched sky-
ward hungrily...*

Matt's fingers tapped impatiently on the keyboard.
Maybe it was the mountains that were complicating
the issue. A change of scenery might work better.

*The sun dropped onto the prairie, cracking like a big
egg and spreading its golden yolk over the tumble-
weeds.*

Too melodramatic and just plain dumb. With a sigh
Matt punched the Delete button, watching as the cursor gobbled the words like a hungry monster. Why was
he having trouble with this one simple sunset?

But he already knew the answer to that question. He
was working to come up with the perfect opening line
for his newest book, *Once a Desperado.* However, in
all honesty, he knew the opening line was the least of
his problems. The whole trouble was that he didn't
know what he was going to say next. The well had run
dry. The train station was empty. There were no bullets in the revolver. And, except for all the annoying
clichés that were tumbling around in his brain, his
mind was blank.

For several long minutes he stared at the blue screen,
hypnotically watching the blinking white line marking the space where the first letter of the first word of
that all-important first sentence should be. He tried to
visualize a prairie, but strings of power lines kept
marring the scenery. His imagination tried to return to
his original idea, and he struggled to summon a mental picture of a rugged mountain range. But all he
could see were the squared peaks of skyscrapers
piercing a smoggy sky.

Matt shook his head, trying to clear his eyes and reorganize his thoughts. How many times had he described a sunset? A mountain? A prairie?

His fingers returned to the keyboard and fiercely tapped out, *The damn sun set*.........

He watched the periods flow across the screen, repeating themselves as his fingers remained pressed against the key. It gave him a certain satisfaction to see the screen filling up, even if it was only with dots.

When the single line of words began to scroll out of sight, he lifted his hands and laced his fingers behind his head.

"I need help," he muttered, standing so abruptly his desk chair rolled across the room. As he walked to the bedroom, he unsnapped the fastener of his jeans and jerked the zipper down. He stepped out of the fashionably faded pants, tossed them across the end of the bed before going to the armoire and selecting a pair of black-checkered bicycle shorts. After pulling them on, he replaced his sweatshirt with a Chicago Bears T-shirt.

One Nike was lying on its side next to his bed. But its mate wasn't being so cooperative. Matt knelt and lifted the edge of the comforter so he could peer under the bed. But other than a few unidentifiable fuzzies and a pair of unclaimed panties, there was nothing hiding under there.

Matt crawled around the room, looking under furniture and behind doors. He wasn't usually this disorganized, but lately nothing seemed to be where it should be, including his shoe *and* his brain.

He finally found the missing sneaker in the bathroom between the toilet and the tub. After shutting the lid, he sat and put on both shoes, tying the long strings tightly so he wouldn't trip on them. The last thing he needed right now was to break his leg…or even worse, his fingers. His editor was expecting a brand new Duke King adventure in the next three months. It was bad enough that Matt couldn't think of a single interesting thing for Duke to do, much less not being able to type it, once inspiration struck.

Exercise was a tried and true stimulant, both for his mind and his body. A jog to the gym a mile from his apartment would flood his brain with oxygen. A couple of hours on the machines and working with weights would occupy his thoughts so his subconscious could go wild and come up with a plot.

And if all else failed, there was sure to be a gorgeous woman in a skintight leotard who would be able to offer him a distraction that would make him forget his editor, his deadline *and* Duke King. At least for the evening.

There was no sign of the sun as he bounded down the steps and began jogging down the street. Thick, gray clouds hung heavily over the buildings, obscuring the top floors of the tallest skyscrapers. It had been a miserable, rainy spring and was showing no sign of change as summer approached. Matt couldn't remember the last time he'd seen the sidewalks dry or made it all the way to the gym without getting splashed from someone driving through a puddle on the street.

A red light stopped him and he jogged in place while he waited for it to change. A low-slung white Jaguar slowed down as it approached the intersection. Its auburn-haired driver gave Matt a bold appraisal, followed by a provocative smile that showed her approval. He responded with a casual wave and a nod of his head. He had a particular weakness for classy redheads with legs long enough to wrap around...

The light changed and Matt gave the retreating white car a last glance before he crossed the street.

Even though he worked out at the gym at least four times a week, Matt made it a point not to get too friendly with any of the other male regulars. Instead of working with a partner as most of the men did, Matt stuck to the weights he could handle alone. He wasn't into power lifting and he wasn't interested in developing a close friendship with a man, so it best served his purpose to keep a comfortable distance between himself and the other men.

The women were a whole different matter. He let them get closer, but only on a physical level. He wasn't any more interested in having a woman for a friend than he was in having a male buddy. The truth was, Matt was a loner. And he liked it that way.

An hour and a half later he finished going through his program and picked up a magazine from a shelf near the stationary bikes. As he pedaled through the computerized cycle, he flipped through the magazine. It was an environmental periodical with beautiful photographs and text that glowingly described the wonders of the great outdoors, which, unfortunately, didn't include any sunsets.

Matt wasn't too impressed. He was a city boy, born and raised near downtown Chicago. Even though he'd done a little traveling back East, Matt was convinced that the Windy City had everything he would ever want out of life.

But as he turned the pages, an advertisement caught his attention. Surrounded by mountains that looked too tall and rough to be real was a picture-perfect ranch. A large, sprawling ranch house and an old-fashioned red barn ringed with whitewashed fences dominated the photo. A caption offered Have A True Western Experience. A closeup of two grizzled cowboys sitting casually on the back of two sleepy-looking horses was further enticement. "Have you ever wondered what it was like to be a cowboy? Join us on trail rides and cattle drives, eat fresh home-cooked meals, participate in a rodeo, sleep under the stars and learn how to square dance. We offer vacations to suit everyone's style whether you want to relax and do nothing or rough it like a real cowboy. Come to the Rocky K Ranch for a Western experience you'll never forget. Make memories that will last a lifetime."

Matt started to turn the page, but there was something about the two old men that kept his attention. With their hats pulled low on their foreheads and the reins held casually in their hands, they looked as much at home on the backs of those horses as Matt did when he was sprawled across his easy chair watching football. That's how Duke King would sit on a horse. And that's how Duke King would wear a cowboy hat. In fact, Duke King had once inherited a ranch very much like the Rocky K, but it had been taken away from him by an evil cattle baron in *Cry of the Lone Wolf*.

The timer clicked off on the exercise bike and Matt dismounted. He tossed the magazine back on the shelf, then bent over and picked it up again. Flipping through to the advertisement, he ripped the page out, folded it and tucked it into his gym bag. It wouldn't hurt to write and see what sort of "Western experiences" they offered. Right now Matt needed something to revive his muse. Perhaps a quick trip to the Rockies might be just what the doctor...or in his case, the editor ordered.

JAMIE KIMBALL sorted the mail with a practiced shuffle. The bills went into a large wire basket and the advertisements went directly into the garbage can. Only the registration letters and the requests for information would receive a quick response.

At least with summer approaching, the reservation and request stack was getting larger. Unfortunately the wire basket wasn't getting any emptier. The expenses of running a working ranch were constant, while the income was unpredictable at best.

Jamie began slitting open the envelopes and dividing them. She would handle the requests after lunch and have them ready to be mailed tomorrow. But the reservations demanded her immediate attention. Unless a miracle happened, it was the reservations that held the future of the Rocky K Ranch.

She flipped through the calendar pages, marking down the dates and names. June, July and August were filling up nicely. As she wrote down a name, she was delighted to note there was only one more opening for June.

As luck would have it, the last two envelopes she opened contained reservations for that last spot. And they both had included checks.

There were only twelve cabins, with six equipped for one or two persons and six larger ones able to comfortably house four or even six if there were small children. Eleven of the cabins were already booked.

Jamie shook her head as she reread the reservations. One was for a young couple from Kansas City who would be on their honeymoon, and the other was a man from Chicago. The newlyweds would fit quite nicely in the small one-room cabin that was left. But then, so would the single man. But the newlyweds would pay almost twice as much money while using the same amount of space.

Jamie glanced again at the man from Chicago's letter. Matt Montana. Somewhere, in the back of her mind, the name rang a bell. Chicago? Matt Montana? No, she couldn't place him. He must have one of those catchy names that seems familiar even when it isn't.

"Too bad, Mr. Matt Montana," she murmured as she returned his letter and deposit check to the envelope and set it aside. She would type a letter explaining that the week he'd requested wasn't available, along with a list of open dates, and get Darlene to drop it at the post office. Hopefully, he would reschedule. Jamie needed him.

Well, not Matt Montana specifically. What Jamie truly needed was a good, well-booked summer's receipts in the bank which meant at least twenty-five Matt Montanas a week during the three-month peak season.

Matt Montana . . . why *did* that name sound so familiar?

Jamie typed the confirmation letters, folded and put them into envelopes addressed to all of the people whose reservations had arrived that day. She also added a list of recommended clothing and supplies and a complete list of activities from which they could choose to fill their days and nights. One of Rocky K's promises was that there would be plenty to do if the guests wanted to stay busy, or they could relax and do nothing at all.

She added the names and the amounts of the deposits to the books, then filled out a deposit slip. If she hurried, she could catch Darlene, the cook, before she went into town to buy groceries this afternoon. It was time-consuming enough that Jamie had to handle all the nit-picking details of reservations and bookkeeping, so she did everything within her power to avoid running errands to town. She begrudged every minute she had to spend confined to the small office. The twenty-mile trip to Telluride wouldn't take long as the crow flies. But since cars were restricted to following the roads as they snaked around the mountains, the drive usually took at least forty minutes each way. And, if Jamie had a choice, she'd rather spend that time holding onto the leather reins of a horse than the plastic circle of a steering wheel.

When she caught Darlene just as she was starting the engine, Jamie decided it must be her lucky day. Already the schedule for June was full, there was a little money in the bank, and she was going to be able to spend a whole afternoon outside in the beautiful spring sunshine. If only she could place that man... Matt Montana. Now where had she heard that name?

"MATT MONTANA!" Buck's fork hung in midair, suspended between his plate and his mouth. "You rejected Matt Montana?"

Jamie looked at her father in amazement. He hadn't been in favor of opening their working ranch to guests and left all the details of running the business end to Jamie. Buck loved the land and the animals and tolerated the guests. Ironically, his gruff, down-to-earth attitude had become a favorite part of the package as people delighted in meeting a man who could "out-cowboy" John Wayne.

And it was evident that Buck was warming to his reputation. His stories of how his ancestors had carved the ranch out of the wild, wild West were growing longer and taking on elements that were closer to fiction than actual history. He no longer avoided the guests, but seemed to enjoy hanging out at the barn, answering the kids' questions and showing remarkable patience with the adults who didn't know the difference between a horse and a mule.

But he had never, to Jamie's recollection, taken an active part in the selection of the guests.

"We're all booked up that week," Jamie explained. "But I offered him several optional dates."

"I can't believe it." Buck set his fork down with a clatter. "You turned down Matt Montana? I accepted all the changes you suggested. I put up with hundreds of greenhorns swarming over my ranch like locusts, spoiling the horses with sugar and leaving the gates open. I even let them take my gosh-darn picture. But the one person *I'd* like to meet, you send away."

Jamie continued to stare at her father in astonishment. The last time he'd been this upset about something was when the representatives from Best of the

West Real Estate had made an offer on the ranch. Who *was* this Matt Montana, anyway?

"Calm down, Dad," she soothed. "Remember your blood pressure."

"Forget my gosh-darn blood pressure. I'm fine. I'm just disappointed," he grumbled. He leaned back in his chair, balancing it on its back legs as he leveled a piercing look at his daughter. "Couldn't we bump somebody? Surely one of those other folks wouldn't mind coming on a different week."

"Dad, why does this mean so much to you?"

Buck idly stroked his bristly beard. "Oh, it means about as much as it would if one of the authors of them romance books you're always reading wanted to come stay here."

Jamie considered his answer, not quite making the connection between her reading preferences and Matt Montana.

Matt Montana. Of course, now she remembered. "That's the guy who writes all those Western books, isn't it?" she asked her father.

Instead of being pleased that she'd finally remembered, Buck seemed almost insulted. "Matt Montana doesn't write *those* Western books," Buck retorted. "He creates masterpieces. His Desperado series is the best stuff I've ever read. That Duke King is a real man."

Jamie dared not point out that the books her father was using for comparison weren't exactly examples of great literature. "The name sounded sort of familiar, but I couldn't put a face to it." She tried to soften the disappointment with a smile. "I'm really sorry, Dad. If I'd known, I would have tried to shuffle the schedule. But I've already sent out the confirmations to everyone else. The only empty space available is in the barn.''

"That's it! I should have thought of that right away.'' Buck's chair settled back on all four legs with a thump. "You haven't mailed the letter to him yet, have you?''

"The letter? Yes, Darlene took it to town with the confirmations.''

"But you have his address, don't you?''

"No, I was in a hurry and didn't write it down.'' At her father's crestfallen look, she hurried to add, "But I offered him some alternate dates and he'll probably contact us again.''

"Dang it! We could have made room for him.''

"Dad, I was just joking about him sleeping in the barn,'' Jamie began. "I realize he must be a man who's spent many nights under the stars in less comfortable places than that, but I wouldn't dream of having a guest . . .''

"Of course he wouldn't have to sleep in the barn,'' Buck stated indignantly. "He could have stayed here in the house with us.''

"Oh, Dad, no.'' Jamie shook her head. "I don't think that would have been a very good idea. We don't know anything about this man. We couldn't invite a complete stranger to stay in our home.''

"Matt Montana is not a complete stranger. I feel I know him through his books,'' Buck defended. "I've got a couple dozen of them in my room. Why don't you read some, and maybe you'll feel more comfortable with him?''

"It would have thrown off our count to have an extra person," she persisted.

"We could have borrowed a horse from the Danielsons, and Darlene could have added an extra potato to the stew," Buck grumbled. "You're the one so all-fired worked up about getting publicity. Just think about how much we'd have once it got out that Matt Montana stayed here. He probably would have set one of his books in this area, maybe even on this ranch. The Rocky K would become so famous we'd be turning people away. By the end of the summer, we could have told those ornery real estate people to stick their contracts where the sun don't..."

"Dad! I get your drift." Jamie threw up her hands to stop him. Once he got wound up on that subject, she wasn't likely to shut him up for hours. And the doctor had warned her he shouldn't get overly excited. Not only that, but her father had hit on a point she hadn't considered. The publicity would have been invaluable.

"Well, it's too late now," she said, sighing, almost as disappointed as her father, now that she was looking at the situation from a purely commercial viewpoint. "When he writes back, I'll make sure we can accommodate him. And I'll try to think of some special activities for him."

"Oh no," her father quickly cut in. "I expect Mr. Montana is an old codger like me, and he'd like spending the evenings in front of the fireplace talking about the Old West with me and Boots."

"Maybe he wanted to stay here to get some peace and quiet."

Buck gave her a knowing look. "We old guys like to talk. There aren't that many of us left anymore. You know, the last real cowboys."

Jamie smiled. If Matt Montana was about her father's age, they would keep each other entertained. She stood and picked up their plates. "Give me a couple of his books, and I'll try to read them in my spare time."

Spare time. That was a joke. She hadn't had any spare time in the last eighteen years since her mother died. But maybe Mr. Matt Montana was the key to a success that would give her and her father a little breathing room.

Besides, how much trouble could the old guy be?

Chapter Two

A fine gray powder swirled behind the convertible, forming an opaque wave that threatened to engulf both man and vehicle if they were to slow down long enough for it to catch up. Matt was determined that wouldn't happen. Small pieces of crushed rock clattered against the underside of the rented Mustang convertible and spun into the tall grass that grew on each side of the narrow road.

As he maneuvered around the sharp curves, Matt smiled, pleased at how well he'd mastered these winding mountain streets. Actually, *street* was too generous a word to describe what was little more than a pathway carved into the wilderness . . . a pathway that was carrying him farther and farther away from civilization.

As much as he hated to consider the possibility, it was very likely that he'd missed a turn. He had a feeling that night came early in this valley, and he sure didn't want to be wandering around after dark.

Matt reached into the pocket of his door and pulled out a road map and the magazine ad. He didn't need to ask for help. If only he could find any sort of landmark, he could figure out where he was and follow the very simple map drawn in the ad. But it had been at least a mile since he'd passed a house and even longer since he'd seen a sign.

With a wary glance at the dust cloud behind him, Matt didn't slow down as he spread the map across the steering wheel. The wind tugged at the paper, whipping the corners and threatening to turn it into a kite. Matt took another curve and glanced down at the map. His gaze darted back and forth as he searched for Ouray and Telluride. Those were the only towns marked on the drawing in the ad, and it showed that the Rocky K Ranch was located on a county road a little to the west of them.

He didn't understand why they hadn't sent him a better map. It was definitely a lack of good organization. Hopefully, this wasn't an omen.

A gust of very cool, persistent mountain air burst through the center of the map and ripped one section from his grasp. Matt grabbed for it with one hand while trying to keep hold and steering around another curve with his other hand.

He didn't see the wagon until it was too late. Automatically he stomped on the brake. The tires locked, trying to grip the road, but the loose rocks propelled the car forward. Matt let the wind rip the pieces of map from his hands as he jerked the steering wheel to the right, trying to head for the ditch.

But as if the covered wagon was made out of a giant magnet instead of old, weathered wood, the black car headed straight for it. In the fleeting seconds that seemed to pass in slow motion before the crash, Matt saw the person sitting on the wagon's seat stare with horror at the rapidly approaching car. A whip cracked over the team of horses' heads, causing them to jump forward. Unfortunately, they had been in the process of making a wide right turn into an open pasture gate and the movement only served to place the wagon more fully in his path. The horses reared and whinnied shrill cries of fear at the unexpected threat.

The convertible's nose plowed into the wagon's big front wheel, shattering it on impact. Long, jagged pieces of spoke scraped across the hood and flew against the windshield. The car slid to a stop, at last, its headlights buried in the box of the wagon.

As the front wheel crumbled, the wagon shifted, favoring its wounded corner, tilting toward the car. For a few seconds it hung suspended, then, with an ancient groan, it collapsed. The driver scrambled to hold on, but the angle of the seat offered no assistance. With a curse that matched the one Matt was muttering, the driver slid down the wooden plank and tumbled onto the hood.

After a complete roll, she came to rest against his windshield. The wind snatched the weathered tan Stetson off her head and sprayed the long, golden strands of her ponytail across the glass.

She was already struggling into a sitting position by the time Matt was able to open the door and jump out.

"Are you hurt?" His gaze swept over her, at least partially relieved that there was no visible blood.

She was gripping her left shoulder and rubbing it. Even though she was obviously in pain, she shook her head. "No, I'm fine."

"Are you sure?"

She slid to the edge of the hood and scowled as she said with unmasked hostility, "What a damn fool thing to do. Didn't you see the wagon?"

"Of course I saw it. Something that big would be hard to miss."

"Obviously!" The woman pushed off the car and landed on her feet, wincing slightly and favoring her right leg as she stalked around him.

As she headed toward the horses, she stripped off her leather gloves and stuffed them in her back pocket. Matt was momentarily distracted by the unconsciously provocative sway of her denim-covered hips and the sassy bounce of the gloves as they hung out of the snug pocket.

"If you've caused one tiny scratch on either of my babies, I'll have you thrown in jail," she stated.

Matt suspected it was no idle threat. He turned his attention to his own vehicle and sputtered another heated round of curses. "Scratches! Just look at my car." He picked up the larger pieces of wood and tossed them to the side of the road, then ran his fingers over the shiny black paint. Each newly discovered scratch or dent brought forth another expletive of increasing passion. "How am I going to explain this to the rental company? They'll never believe me. Hell, *I* wouldn't believe me. I can just see their expressions when I tell them I had a collision with a covered wagon."

The woman didn't pay any attention to his rantings as she quieted the nervous horses and checked them for injuries.

Matt vaulted over the damaged hood and strode over to her. She didn't so much as glance in his direction as she worked with the buckles of the harness.

"You were taking up the whole road," he accused, pacing back and forth beside her. "You saw me coming. Why didn't you move that thing out of the way?"

She released the horses from the center shaft of the wagon and led them away from the wreckage before she answered. "I was making a perfectly legal turn. It's not like they installed rack and pinion steering on that model of covered wagon." She marched up to him, not stopping until she was only a couple of feet away. With her feet braced stiffly and her hands on her hips, she confronted him with a fierceness that surprised him. "And there aren't any signal lights, either. If you hadn't been driving like a bat out of hell, you'd have been able to keep control of your car."

He leveled his best withering glare at her. "I'm *always* in control."

Her blue eyes glittered dangerously as she glared up at him. Slowly, eloquently, she let her gaze drop. She took her time studying every inch of his body from the top of his dark, wind-blown hair to the tips of his shockingly expensive, brand-new cowboy boots. It took every ounce of his masculine pride to keep from shifting under her critical inspection. When her gaze returned to his, he was annoyed and a little uncomfortable to see censure and even a touch of amusement in her eyes.

"You're not from around here." She stated it as a fact rather than a question. "The rule of the road is whoever's bigger or driving in front has the right of way. Obviously, my wagon qualified."

He raked his fingers through his hair, pushing it back from his forehead. This woman was the most annoying creature he'd ever met. He was the one who should be angry. She was completely at fault. And yet she wasn't accepting the slightest measure of blame. "What sort of hick civilization is this? I feel as if I've driven through a time tunnel."

She snorted wryly. "Why not? You tried driving through everything else!"

"It wasn't like I had a real choice."

"There was the ditch," she commented with an irritating calm.

"This is a public road," he sputtered. "I don't think it's too much to expect a lane to drive in, or at least space to pass. You were spread all over the place."

Her hands clenched into fists, and she took a step forward. Matt stood his ground, but he was so sure she was going to slug him that he braced himself.

Instead she continued to hold his gaze locked in hers as she accused, "I was working...not cruising the back roads, looking for an unsuspecting victim."

"You were working?" His chuckle was dry and intentionally insulting. "I didn't realize there was a big call for wagon drivers. Was this a college course or did you go to the Donner Party trade school? You sure didn't learn it at charm school."

"*I* wasn't the one who ran into a vehicle the size of a small house," she pointed out, her own lips curving into a contentious half smile.

In spite of his determination not to let her get to him, Matt felt an angry flush rise to his cheekbones. She was standing so close to him that he could see the black spikes radiating from her pupils through the pale blue irises of her eyes, reminding him of the spokes of the broken wagon wheel. The wind tossed her long, straight ponytail over her shoulder and twisted loose tendrils of spun-gold hair across her face. The wind also blew a light, fresh floral scent to his flared nostrils, but he couldn't determine whether it was from the fields of wildflowers or from the woman in front of him. Somehow he guessed her perfume of choice would be eau de horse.

His gaze drifted lower, distracted by the swell of tanned skin visible above the low, circular neckline of her yellow tank top. The women in his books often had bosoms that heaved in frustration or indignation, but he'd never, until that moment, actually seen one do it.

And what a bosom it was. Even still caught up in his own indignation he was beginning to notice that there was a very pretty young woman under all those bristles and thorns. Too bad they had met under such unpleasant circumstances. He'd heard plenty of stories about the warmth and generosity of farmers' daughters.

"What the hell . . . er heck's going on here?"

Matt and the woman turned to look at a man who had ridden up on a rangy sorrel gelding. Leaning back in his saddle he surveyed the mess through squinted eyes.

"The horses are okay, Pa," the woman said.

"Pa?" Matt murmured. "I take it this man's your father."

"I wouldn't call him Pa if he wasn't," she muttered back.

"How very 'Bonanza'," Matt couldn't resist commenting.

She responded with a drop-dead glare, then whirled and walked to where her father was waiting.

"The wheel's ruined," she declared. "I'm not sure we can have it repaired in time for the wagon train on Monday. And there could be structural damage, too."

The saddle creaked as the old man swung down. His long legs retained the rounded shape of the horse as he walked to where the car was planted into the wagon. He ran one hand over the bleached wooden panel of its side before saying, "This baby's built like a tank. I don't think a little bitty car like this one could do it any permanent damage."

"How about the car!" Matt exclaimed, amazed that in the midst of the broken wood and dented metal, all they could see was the wagon. "This car'll never be the same. There's probably even damage to the frame. It was like hitting a brick wall." He shook his head in exasperation. "I should have taken out the extra insurance."

"They don't offer insurance for stupidity," the woman remarked with a pointed glance in his direction.

"Well, we aren't solving anything by standing out here in the middle of the road arguing about this," the old man said. "It's going to be dark soon, and we have to get both these vehicles off the road before someone else comes along and gets hurt."

The woman's hand automatically went to her shoulder, and Matt noticed a dark bruise was already beginning to purple her smooth skin. But her father didn't notice as he extended his hand toward Matt.

"I guess if my daughter's not going to make the introductions, I will. My name's Buck Kimball."

Matt shook the man's hand. "I'm Matt Montana, and I was on my way..."

"Matt Montana!" Buck's eyes widened as much as his wrinkled face would allow. "Not *the* Matt Montana?"

"Well, I'm not sure which Matt Montana you mean, but if it's the one who writes Western novels, then yes, that's me."

"Hot dang!" Buck exclaimed. "It's sure a pleasure to meet you, son, although I'd always pictured you as older."

"I hear that a lot," Matt said. "Actually, I feel I've aged a dozen or so years today."

"I'm sorry about this. Sometimes my daughter can be a little too temperamental. You know how women are."

Jamie cast her father a startled look, then tossed her head, sending her thick, honey-colored ponytail tumbling down her back.

"But what are you doing here?" Buck continued. "I thought you weren't coming."

"Of course I was coming," Matt answered. "I sent a check along with my registration form. I thought it was all arranged."

"I sent your check back," the woman said. "We were booked solid for next week."

Matt shook his head. "I never got your letter or my check. I thought it was a pretty careless way to run a business not to have some form of confirmation."

"You weren't confirmed because we can't accommodate you," she responded.

"Of course we can," Buck interrupted. "Like I said before, we'll find him a place. Gosh darn, he can even stay in our house." He turned to his daughter. "You can clean out the spare room."

"But, Pa..."

"I'm sure all the other guests will be as excited as I am that Matt's going to join us. He can tell stories around the campfire about Duke King and..."

"Uh...no, actually, I'd rather not have to tell any stories," Matt broke in. "This is the first vacation I've taken in five years and I sort of wanted to relax and get away from Duke for a while."

"That's okay, son," Buck agreed. "You've come to the right place to relax and have a good time. Jamie and I will see to that, won't we?" He gave his daughter a meaningful look that silenced the protests that were still forming on her lips.

The woman Matt now knew was named Jamie gave him one last mutinous glare before she began walking toward the horses.

"I'll ride the team back to the ranch and send Boots out here with the truck so he can haul the wagon home," she said, tossing the words over her shoulder as if she couldn't bear standing around with the two men any longer.

Both men watched her go, each looking at her with a completely different perspective. Buck noticed the skillful way she handled the horses and the ease with which she vaulted onto one of them. Matt noticed the way her slender legs, left bare by a pair of cutoff shorts, spread across the horse's broad back.

"Don't worry about her," Buck said to Matt. "She'll come around."

Matt smiled, the first real smile of the afternoon.

Chapter Three

Duke gathered the reins in his hands and swung into the saddle.

"Please stay," Lucy pleaded. "I've never met a man like you."

He looked down at the full pale breasts almost spilling out of the partially unbuttoned nightgown. How well he remembered how those heavy orbs filled his hands. He still ached from the hours he'd spent making love to that body last night. As tempting as it was to share her bed for a few more days, Duke knew it was time to move on.

He leaned down and caressed her cheek, letting one golden curl wrap around his finger. "You're a good woman, Lucy. Someday a man will come along who won't have to leave." He straightened in the saddle, anxious to be on his way. "But that man won't be me. I'm not the kind to settle down."

"I won't tie you down," Lucy cried, the tears spilling out of her baby-blue eyes. "You can come and go as you please. Just please don't leave me. I can't live without you."

"Sorry, Lucy. I'm just not a one-woman man." He
touched the brim of his hat. *"Goodbye."* His heels
dug into Thunderbolt's sleek black flanks as he pulled
the reins to the right. The horse whirled on its hind
legs, rearing slightly before falling into a ground-
eating gallop that quickly took Duke King out of Dry
Gulch and on to another adventure and another
warm, willing woman.

Jamie stared at the last sentence of the chapter as if
she couldn't quite believe what she had read. *Warm,
willing woman!* What sort of jerk was Duke King?
The same sort of jerk as Matt Montana. It was easy to
see where he got his inspiration.

She flung the book across the room, aiming for the
garbage can, but missing. *Desperado of Dry Gulch*
landed against the wall and slid to the hardwood floor.
Jamie groaned and leaned back against her pillows.

How could her father like such trash? Even though
he wasn't the most sensitive, nineties' man in the
world, surely he didn't hold women in contempt like
the fictitious Duke King and the very nonfictitious
Matt Montana. On the other hand, her father had
never quite been able to hide his disappointment that
his only child hadn't been a boy. But he'd never been
intentionally cruel about it.

Jamie had long ago accepted that her father loved
her, but would probably never appreciate all she did
for him and the ranch. Since she did it because she
wanted to and not to impress anyone, recognition
didn't really matter.

What mattered at the moment was that her father
had ignored her feelings and invited that man to sleep
under this very roof. What a nut case! He'd probably

kill them in their beds...or just torture them to death by reading passages from his books.

Matt Montana had done everything he could to intimidate her, probably because he was accustomed to having people fall at his feet once they found out he was the world-famous author. But even if she had known his identity, she wouldn't have backed down. The accident had been all his fault, and she refused to take an ounce of the blame.

And now she was going to have to put up with his insufferable arrogance for a whole week. Lord, the publicity had better be worth it!

Jamie picked up the romance novel on her nightstand, opened it to her bookmark and tried to get her mind off Matt, Duke and every other domineering male. What she wanted was a sweet, funny, understanding guy who could be her best friend, sharing life's problems and taking his turn cooking dinner, just like the heroes in her favorite books. Jamie's fantasy wasn't to be dominated, but to be cherished. Surely there was a man out there somewhere who was perfect for her.

But at twenty-eight, Jamie was beginning to have her doubts. If Mr. Right or Mel Gibson . . . yes, especially Mel Gibson . . . was going to ride up on a white horse and carry her away, he'd better hurry up.

Jamie's stomach growled, reminding her that she'd missed supper that evening. By the time her father and Boots had gotten the crippled wagon into the equipment shed, it had been well after dark. Her father had left to spend time with the few guests who had arrived early while Jamie and Boots stayed with the wagon to assess the damage.

They'd worked together to mend the box, well aware that they were racing the clock. Tomorrow the rest of the guests would arrive, and they would require almost every spare minute of Jamie's time. Everyone would be matched to a horse, given a quick riding lesson and taken on a very brief tour of the ranch. Then Sunday would be a light activity day, allowing the guests time to get used to the altitude, the animals and each other, before the different groups set off on their chosen adventure on Monday.

Her stomach growled again, and Jamie glanced at the clock. It was almost midnight. Tomorrow would be a long day and she needed her sleep. But she felt restless and tense, almost as if she was waiting for something to happen. Something important. Something that would change her life forever. She wished she knew if that change would be for better or worse.

Jamie gave up on her book and returned it to her nightstand. She couldn't go to sleep while she was hungry, so she might as well get a bite to eat, then go over the menus Darlene had prepared and check the supply pantry. With an extra guest added to the already full registration, she didn't want to run short.

As soon as she reached the bottom of the stairs she noticed there was a light on in the kitchen. So, Buck couldn't sleep, either. He, too, must be concerned about the arrival of so many guests. It was the first time they had been booked solid since opening the ranch to the public two years ago. How sweet that he was nervous.

But when she reached the kitchen, her bare feet slid to a stop on the waxed linoleum floor. The man standing at the sink getting a drink of water was definitely not her father.

His broad tanned shoulders seemed to fill the room. Muscles rippled beneath the bronzed skin as he leaned forward on the countertop, one arm braced, while he rolled the frosted glass against his forehead. For several seconds the only sound in the room was the ice tumbling around inside the glass as Jamie watched, secretly admiring the man's gorgeous body in spite of her intense dislike for him. After all, she rationalized, a person could appreciate the beauty and awesome power of a thunderstorm without wanting to actually be struck by a bolt of lightning.

A pair of snug jeans hugged his long legs, but hung loosely around his hips. As he turned, Jamie's gaze was drawn to the open V at the waistband where the top button hadn't been fastened, enticing her imagination more than she cared to admit.

He was obviously startled by her presence and pushed away from the sink, standing tall and straight as she forced her inspection upward, over the taut ridges of his stomach to the muscular swell of his chest. Her attention wandered to the flex of his arm as he lifted the glass to his lips.

Okay, so he had a great body. Big deal. Any man, with a little exercise, could have bulging muscles. Unfortunately no amount of exercise could help develop a guy's deficient personality.

His Adam's apple bobbed as he swallowed, then he lowered the glass. For a few seconds her eyes focused on his lips: sensuous, strong lips, still moist from his drink.

Okay, so he had a great body *and* fantastic lips. Lots of men had nice lips. Unfortunately, once he opened them they lost all their appeal.

She was unreasonably pleased to see his nose wasn't perfect. A crooked bump on the bridge implied that it had come in contact with a solid obstacle at some point in his life. Of course, he could have broken it while playing some sport, but Jamie was more inclined to believe he'd been his same old unpleasant self to someone else, and they hadn't showed the restraint she had. There had been several moments that afternoon when she would have loved to hit him in that arrogant nose herself.

However, try as she would, she could find no fault with his hair. Thick, straight and shiny, it was as black as the moonless night outside the window. Tousled from a restless sleep or from rough fingers hastily dragged through it, a heavy lock tumbled across his forehead.

She had avoided his eyes, saving them for last. During their earlier encounter, they'd remained hidden behind mirrored sunglasses. It had fueled her anger when she'd looked up at him and had seen only her own reflection staring back at her. Now she peered directly into his eyes, not knowing what sort of demons he'd been hiding.

With his dark, Italian coloring she would have guessed his eyes would be a deep brown. She was a little startled to find they were, instead, a beautiful shade of blue. They reminded her of a midnight-blue crayon that had always been one of her favorite colors when she was a child, an odd color that could be either warm or cool depending on the picture. Jamie could easily imagine how those eyes could chill a person to the bone. It was more difficult to see how they could generate warmth. But as she boldly met his gaze, she was pulled to those fathomless eyes, fascinated by the intelligence she saw there.

Of all the qualities of which Matt Montana could boast... and she was certain he boasted more often than the law should allow... intelligence was the last she would have matched with his behavior and the literature, to use the term loosely, he produced.

Okay, so he had a great body, fantastic lips and fascinating eyes that promised at least a degree of intelligence. Funny how she hadn't noticed any of those things when they had stood face-to-face in the middle of the road. He had a personality that was so annoying that it overshadowed every good quality. Whatever attraction she might have to the man was neutralized by his macho attitude, both after the accident and in the book she had read. Jamie had no doubt that Matt Montana wrote what he knew... and Duke King was obviously an older, but not wiser version of his creator.

"See anything you like?" he asked, an impudent twinkle brightening his eyes.

It was amazing how quickly and almost effortlessly he could arouse her temper. Jamie was usually the peacemaker, arbitrating arguments between her father, Boots, Darlene and, occasionally, guests. Her calm soothed the flightiest horse and defused the most hostile situation. But there was something about Mr. Montana that pushed all the wrong buttons.

"No wonder you couldn't sleep," she retorted. "With an ego the size of yours, it must be uncomfortable to lie down."

"It wasn't my ego you were looking at."

Jamie's mouth opened to disagree, but, for once, she couldn't think of a single snappy comeback. Her only defense was to ignore his implication. With a toss of her head that sent her long, blond hair swirling in her wake, she turned her back toward him and took a glass from the cabinet. She struggled to control her righteous indignation as she walked to the refrigerator and poured herself a glass of orange juice. By the time she took a drink and slowly pivoted to face him again, she was back in control of her emotions.

"Help yourself to whatever's in the refrigerator," she informed him. "Good night, Mr. Montana." Walking with measured poise, she exited the room.

Jamie was halfway up the stairs when her poise failed her. The steps she had climbed almost every day of her life sabotaged her graceful retreat. Her bare toes misjudged the width of the wooden stair and slipped off the edge. The sudden jarring movement caused the juice to slosh out of the glass and splash onto her feet and the steps.

For a moment she considered leaving the puddle to dry rather than return to the kitchen. But realistically she knew it would be easier to clean it up now instead of leaving it until it became a sticky mess. Besides, someone else might slip and hurt themselves.

Swallowing her lack of enthusiasm with having to see Matt again so soon, she walked back into the kitchen. Expecting to find him standing arrogantly by the sink, she was surprised to see him sitting at the small kitchen table, his head resting on the cradle of his arms.

It was such a vulnerable position, so unlike the cocky self-confidence he usually displayed, that Jamie wasn't sure what to do next.

"Are you okay?" she asked.

He immediately straightened and tried to look as if nothing was wrong, but he couldn't quite chase the pain from his eyes. "Sure, I'm fine," he answered with a bravado that was transparently false.

"You are not," she countered.

"I never get sick."

"There's a first time for everything." She put her glass on the table and walked up to him. "And, if it's all the same to you, I'd rather you didn't do anything awkward like dying while you're here on my ranch."

She reached out to check his forehead for a temperature, but her hand hesitated a few inches over his head. It was as if there was a force field of virility surrounding him. She could feel it pulsing through her, drawing her closer.

His hair felt like silk against her fingers as she pushed it aside. He sat perfectly still, meeting her eyes with a steamy look that brought a wave of fevered heat coursing through her own body. Even now, with the pain he was trying so hard to deny, dulling his eyes, there was a cockiness in the tilt of his head and the arch of his black eyebrows.

Jamie's heart fluttered in her chest at the intensity of his gaze as it focused on her, hypnotizing her like a cobra preparing to strike. A warning flashed through her brain, telling her to run and hide before it was too late.

Too late? Too late for what? Jamie never ran and hid from anything and had no idea where that bizarre idea was coming from now.

Scoffing at her own skittishness, she flattened her hand against his forehead. There was nothing intimate in the gesture . . . and yet Jamie's palm tingled as it pressed against his skin.

She would have jerked her hand away, but there was a subtle change in his expression. His eyes widened slightly and his air of confidence was replaced by a look of surprise, followed quickly by a hint of confusion. He started to pull away, but then his eyes drifted closed, and he leaned against the pressure of her fingers.

The strange feelings that were tumbling around inside her shifted direction. Fortunately the emotion he was evoking was one with which she was very familiar . . . that of nurse and nurturer. If anyone or anything, from her father all the way down the ladder to the newest baby chicken, got sick or had a problem, Jamie was always the one to handle the situation. Now that Matt seemed willing to finally forgo his macho pride and admit that he wasn't feeling well, Jamie began to feel more comfortable.

"You have a headache, don't you?" she asked.

"That's an understatement. It feels like a herd of stampeding buffalo are trapped inside my skull."

Jamie resisted the urge to point out that all the shouting Matt had done earlier had probably brought on the added pressure in his brain. But as he glanced up at her through a thick, black fringe of lashes that were surely the envy of every woman who saw them, Jamie couldn't help but feel sorry for him. Even so, she wouldn't put it past him to have gotten a lot of mileage out of those sexy lashes and that poor-little-puppy-dog look. Jamie could easily imagine how a woman who hadn't seen the *real* Matt Montana might be completely taken in by his pitiful expression. She wondered how many women had pulled his dark, handsome head into the cradle of their bosoms...and wound up in his bed that night.

Well, she had plenty of opportunities to mess up her life and make a fool of herself without Matt's help. He might have forced his way onto her guest list, but he would never wind up in her bed.

"I'll get you some aspirin," she offered, suddenly anxious to break the physical and emotional contact and to put some distance between herself and Matt.

"Thanks," he murmured as if it was a word he wasn't accustomed to using.

Jamie went to the cabinet beside the stove and took down a bottle of tablets, then carried the bottle and his glass of water to the table. Matt was leaning forward, his elbow braced on the table as he massaged his forehead with his fingertips.

He took the two aspirins she offered, washing them down with a big gulp of water. Jamie started to turn away, but he grabbed her arm.

"I need more," he said, his voice low and husky.

So here it came...the sales pitch. Jamie braced herself for his proposition. "More what?" she challenged.

The corners of his lips twitched as if they wanted to smile, but didn't quite have the strength. "More aspirins," he answered. "I don't think I'm up to anything else. But I'll take a rain check."

She dropped the plastic container on the table and pulled away. "That isn't one of the extracurricular activities offered in the brochure."

"Too bad." One dark eyebrow arched provocatively. "It always makes me feel better."

Jamie met his gaze with a poise she wasn't feeling. There was something about this man that rattled her concentration. "I thought you said you didn't get sick."

"I didn't say it made me *well*...I said it made me *feel* better."

Jamie shrugged. "You're going to have to settle for aspirins while you're here. When you get back to Chicago, you can *feel* as good as you want...as often as you want. Once you leave this ranch, it's no business of mine."

Matt's head dropped back onto the table, cradled by his crossed arms. "I would really like to continue this discussion...but I feel too rotten to argue right now." He groaned. "Somehow I always thought I'd be killed on the streets of Chicago..."

"By a jealous husband, no doubt," Jamie commented.

He didn't bother trying to deny the possibility. "But I never thought I'd die on a dude ranch in the wild, wild West."

"It's sort of poetic justice, isn't it? Your alter ego, Dude King..."

"It's *Duke,*" he corrected.

She shrugged. "Okay, Duke King has conquered the West, dodging bullets and leaving brokenhearted women in his dust."

Matt rolled his head to one side and squinted up at her. "A little sympathy would be nice, you know. It's not going to be good publicity for me to die here on your ranch."

Jamie walked back to the cabinet and took down another bottle and opened it. "I'm sorry," she said with as much sincerity as she could muster. "I know you feel really awful. But I have every confidence you're going to survive."

"How can you be so sure?"

"Because no one's ever died of altitude sickness. It hits a lot of people when they stay in the mountains, and I recognize the symptoms." She shook a few colored disks from the container and held them out to him on her open palm. "Here, chew these. They'll make you feel better."

Without lifting his head, he eyed the large round tablets skeptically. "Those are Rolaids. I don't have an upset stomach."

"Trust me, they work."

Matt's expression very clearly told her he *didn't* trust her. But he took the tablets and popped them in his mouth. "I guess they can't make me feel any worse."

Jamie smiled, pleased to have the upper hand, even though she suspected it would only be temporary. All too soon, he'd be back to his old, obnoxious self. She tore off a handful of paper towels, picked up her glass of juice and headed for the doorway.

"You really should try to get some sleep now," she told him. "It gets pretty noisy around here after day-break. The cabins are farther from the barns, so the guests there can sleep in. But this house is the center of activity."

"No problem. I won't survive until morning." His voice was muffled in the hollow circle of his arms.

Jamie stopped and glanced over her shoulder at him. She truly believed his ailment was as she'd diagnosed it. Only a little time and another dose of Rolaids would help.

Still, he was her guest...sort of. Well, not *her* guest, but certainly a guest of the ranch. It was her duty to make sure he was settled.

"Oh, shoot," she grumbled, tempted to use a much stronger curse. She walked back to the table and set her glass and towel down. "Well, come on, cowboy. I'll help you to your room."

He let her pull him into a standing position and draped his arm around her shoulder. Jamie staggered slightly under his weight and put her arm around his waist to steady herself. Her hand unintentionally slipped inside the loose waistband of his jeans. As she felt the jut of his hipbone, she forced herself not to remove her hand because she didn't want him to know how much the feel of his naked flesh beneath her fingers affected her.

"There's nothing wrong with your legs," she reminded him, suspecting he was overplaying his illness and hoping her voice didn't sound as shaky as she felt.

Instead of shifting his weight off her, he leaned more heavily against her. "All of a sudden I feel real weak," he said, but a roguish gleam broke through the shadow of pain in his eyes as he gazed down at her.

Jamie shook her head in amazement. "You're unbelievable. I've heard the term 'Italian stallion,' but until I met you, I thought it was a joke."

"We Italian stallions don't take our role as the most romantic men in the world lightly."

"All our stallions sleep in the barn."

"I've heard making love in the hay can be very sensual."

"Maybe for men, because they don't have to lie on the uncomfortable, sticky stuff," Jamie scoffed. "You've been reading...or writing too much fiction."

One eyebrow arched in a silent challenge as he responded. "It sounds like you're speaking from experience."

"Don't sound so surprised. You're not the first man to suggest a tryst in the barn."

"Which you apparently accepted."

Jamie shrugged noncommittally. "I don't tryst and tell."

"Well, if I survive this headache, I'll check out the barn for myself."

"You'll have to do it alone," she commented. "There aren't any single women registered here for this week's activities."

"You're single."

She shifted, uncomfortably aware that she was wearing only a light gown and robe as his warm, bare skin seemed to burn through the thin layers. But no matter how she moved, she could still feel way too much of his body against hers. In fact, her movements only made it worse as her breast brushed across his ribcage.

"Yes, but I'm not interested," she lied, desperately wishing it was the truth.

Jamie stopped at the doorway of his bedroom and let her arm drop from his waist.

"This is as far as I go."

Again, he gave her a provocative look. "I was hoping you'd tuck me in...." He turned and let his hands trail along her arms until they gripped her shoulders. Slowly he leaned toward her. "And kiss me goodnight."

The words were barely a whisper, gently brushing across her face. Jamie's heart slid to a stop. She would have fled, but her bare feet had grown to the spot. Desperately she tried to remember all the reasons why she couldn't let him kiss her. He was loud, obnoxious, cocky, arrogant and had obviously never heard the word *no* from a woman. The last thing in the world she needed was to get involved with a guest...especially this particular guest.

And yet, standing so close to him, breathing in his heady masculine scent, her line of vision completely filled with his fantastic body, her common sense was wavering. Before it deserted her completely, she said, "You're a big boy. You don't need to be tucked in. I'm not your mother."

Matt's hands tightened painfully on her shoulders, then he abruptly let her go. Jamie staggered back a step, amazed at the transformation of his expression from playfully flirtatious to coldly distant. His fingers lifted to his temples, massaging them fiercely as if he could rub the pain away.

"Good night," he said, his eyes again darkened with pain. "Thanks for the pills...and the help to my room."

Jamie was confused, but grateful for his sudden change of attitude. She'd been saved at the last minute from making a mistake she would probably regret for the rest of her life. With one last glance at his dangerously handsome face and hard, muscular body, she breathed a sigh of relief...or was it disappointment?

Chapter Four

He would have covered all bets against it, but he survived the night. It came as quite a surprise to Matt, considering how bad he'd felt when he went to bed. As annoying as it was to admit it, Jamie had been right about the illness and the medication.

And she'd been right about something else ... the morning noise was enough to wake the dead.

Matt rolled over onto his stomach on the bed and pulled the extra pillow over his head. Even through the layer of feathers, he could hear the roosters crowing, the cows mooing, the horses neighing, the dogs barking and the ear-splitting bray of a donkey. It sounded like feeding time at the zoo.

Matt longed for the comforting hum of traffic that was usually outside his window at this time of the day. He had no problem sleeping through the racing motors, honking horns, sirens and even an occasional backfire. But these animal noises were impossible to ignore.

He finally gave up and sat up on the edge of the bed. A brisk breeze blew in the open window, billowing the lace curtains like sails on a boat. The jagged peaks of the Rockies, most still wearing their winter coat of snow, were incredibly close, dominating the crystal-blue sky. Matt breathed in a deep breath of the mountain air and collapsed in a coughing fit as the cold air filled his lungs. Deciding those lungs didn't know how to process pure, clean air, Matt shut the window.

By the time he showered, shaved, dressed and went downstairs, Darlene was clearing the dirty dishes off the kitchen table. She barely glanced at him as she passed on her way to the sink.

"You missed breakfast," she stated and gave a pointed look at the cow-shaped clock on the wall. "They eat early here on the ranch."

Matt couldn't ignore the fragrance of homemade biscuits and bacon that still clung to the air. After last night's delicious supper, he knew Darlene was a good cook, even if she had all the warmth of an Arctic iceberg. Deciding it was time to pour on his potent Italian charm, he picked up a couple of dirty plates and followed Darlene to the sink.

"I didn't think I'd be hungry after everything I ate last night. I'm used to eating in some five-star restaurants, but that was a fine meal you prepared."

Darlene's dour expression never changed. "City food. They don't know anything about good cooking in those places."

Matt turned his head so she wouldn't see his confident smile. Obviously she was weakening, and it would be only a matter of minutes before she was standing at that stove, scrambling some farm-fresh eggs and buttering a half dozen hot buttermilk biscuits. "I get tired of eating out almost every day. Ever since I read about those home-cooked meals that were advertised in the ad, my mouth's been watering in anticipation.''

Darlene passed him again and picked up the final load of dishes. As she placed them in the sink, she peered at him over the top of her glasses. "Good. Lunch'll be ready at noon. Don't be late or you'll miss that, too."

Matt's smile faded as the full meaning of her words soaked in. He stood helplessly, looking at her back as she turned her full attention to the pile of dishes. His stomach protested loudly, but since there wasn't a restaurant or even a 7-Eleven for God only knew how many miles, he didn't have much of a choice. She'd made her point, though. He would certainly keep a closer watch on the clock around meal times.

He inhaled another deep breath since the odor of food would have to hold him for the next four hours. Feeling like a stranger in a foreign land, he knew he would have to accept that at least for the moment, there was nothing he could do to change things. "Well, set a place for me," he told her, "because I'll be here on time, and I'll be hungry."

Matt pulled on the black Stetson he'd bought for this trip and headed for the door. His hand was on the knob when he stopped and added, "I really meant what I said about your cooking. I guarantee I won't miss another of your meals."

He turned the knob and was pulling the door open when he heard Darlene say, "There's a couple biscuits left in the oven. They're probably cold, but you can have them. I was going to feed them to the dog, anyway."

Feeling unreasonably blessed, Matt strode across to the oven and took out the pan. There were only two biscuits left, but he'd ordered perfectly prepared prime rib with less anticipation than when he wrapped the biscuits in a paper towel and left the kitchen. The first biscuit, even without butter and jelly, seemed to melt in his mouth.

A spotted dog stood and stretched. Disturbed from his nap in the cool dirt of the flower bed by the back porch, he wagged his tail and began trotting after Matt.

"Don't get your hopes up, old boy," Matt told the dog. "This biscuit is all that stands between me and starvation. You've probably got a bowl of dog chow or a yummy bone stashed somewhere."

The dog's long, drooling tongue curled across his upper lip as he continued to stare covetously at the biscuit in Matt's hand.

"Look, I'm still recovering from some kind of goofy illness." Matt glanced down at the mixed-breed mutt and couldn't help but think that the dog didn't look all that healthy, either. But Matt was determined not to share his sparse breakfast and tried very hard to ignore the creature as they headed toward the corrals.

Matt was taking a bite out of the biscuit when he rounded the corner of the barn and was nearly run down by a very large horse.

The animal reared and Matt automatically retreated. Unfortunately the dog had stopped at Matt's heels. The mutt's body became a solid obstacle that tackled Matt at the knees, sending him tumbling backward.

The confusion excited the horse even more and she pawed the dirt of the yard. From his prone position, the animal looked as big as a dinosaur. Her iron-shod hooves flashed dangerously close to some very delicate parts of Matt's body, and he rolled off to one side, out of reach of the vicious equine.

"Feeling better, Mr. Montana?" a feminine voice asked.

Matt adjusted his gaze from the still-dancing hooves to the woman sitting on the horse's back. He hated how perky and wide awake she looked when he felt like he still needed a few more hours of sleep. "Well, I was, until I was practically trampled."

Jamie swung out of the saddle and held out her hand. "Sorry. Stormy's always a little frisky first thing in the morning."

"I wish I could say the same about myself," Matt muttered as he ignored her outstretched hand and stood up without help.

"At least you woke up before noon. I lost five bucks on that one."

Matt swatted the dust off his jeans and frowned at the scuff on the toe of his new boots. "You bet that I wouldn't get up until after noon?"

Jamie's blue eyes twinkled. "The way you were snoring this morning, I thought it was a sure thing."

"I don't snore," Matt retorted, but then his confidence faltered. "Do I?"

"I've heard worse." She gathered the reins in her hand, fit her foot into the stirrup and swung back into the saddle.

Matt's eyes squinted as he looked up at her. She made it sound as if she was very familiar with the sleeping habits of many men. For some reason, that thought made him furious. She wouldn't even let him kiss her, and yet she'd slept with lots of other men.

But then she hadn't slept with him, and she'd heard him snore. Suspiciously he asked, "So how'd you happen to hear me? Your room is down the hall from mine."

One shoulder lifted in a shrug. "Oh, I looked in on you when I went down to breakfast." She gave him a taunting smile. "I needed to know whether or not my diagnosis was correct...or whether I needed to call the coroner."

Matt felt his jaw drop, but he refused to give her the satisfaction of goading him. "Yeah, well, you could have done me the favor of waking me so I wouldn't have missed breakfast. If it hadn't been for Darlene giving me these biscuits..."

"You missed breakfast and Darlene gave you some biscuits?" Jamie echoed. "Wow, she must really like you. Usually she'll feed them to T-bone before she'll let someone be late to a meal."

Matt suddenly realized he was no longer holding the biscuit. He and Jamie looked around just in time to see the dog, whose name was apparently T-bone, gobble it up from the ground where it had fallen. With a satisfied wag of his long tail and a look at Matt that seemed to say the biscuit had been delicious, the dog trotted away.

At the sound of Jamie's laughter, Matt snorted, "I hope you're happy. It's still..." He glanced at his watch. "Good God, it's still three and a half hours until lunch."

She reached into one of the saddlebags that were draped over Stormy's broad rump and pulled out an apple. "Here, this should hold you. I always keep a stash of food for just this kind of emergency."

She tossed the apple to him and he deftly caught it. "Thanks," he said. "That makes the score two to two."

"Two to two?"

"Yes, you've saved my life twice and tried to kill me twice."

Her smile was wry and held a hint of a challenge. "The week's just begun."

Stormy fidgeted beneath her, the horse's patience apparently exhausted. Her hooves danced in place, stirring up a whirlwind of dust. Jamie tightened the reins and the big dappled-gray mare tossed her head in protest before obeying the pressure against her neck. She took a few steps sideways, then trotted past Matt, so close that the long, coarse hairs of her tail slapped the man's face.

Matt didn't know how she did it, but he would have bet Jamie planned her exit exactly that way.

"I WANT TO WELCOME everyone to the Rocky K Ranch." Jamie sat on a now placid Stormy in the middle of the corral.

All thirty-seven guests were assembled inside the fence, either leaning against it or sitting on the heavy rails. Matt and Buck stood on the outside of the fence off to the side as Jamie continued her orientation speech.

"I know some of you are experienced riders, but, for the sake of those who haven't spent much time around horses, I want to go over a few of the more important details you should remember. Most of our horses are quarter horses which are an American breed developed for ranch work in the 1700s. They're sure-footed and intelligent, so trust their instincts. Everyone should stay together, but if you should get lost, tie the reins loosely around the saddle horn and let your horse find his way home. I guarantee he'll get you back here by the most direct route.

"These horses weigh about a half ton each, but, luckily they are convinced that you're the boss. There are several things you should do to keep control, and one of the most important is..."

"So how'd you sleep last night?" Buck turned his back to the fence as he spoke to Matt.

"What did your daughter tell you?" Matt couldn't hide his annoyance. How like a woman not to be able to keep her mouth shut. They were like vultures, circling, waiting for a man to show any sign of weakness so they could swoop in to strip him of his masculinity. That was why Matt had tried to keep his illness to himself.

Buck gave Matt a curious look. "My daughter? What does she have to do with how you slept?"

Now it was Matt's turn to study the older man. One of the things he avoided at all costs was angry fathers...especially when he hadn't touched their daughters. And it wasn't often that Matt could respond with righteous innocence. "She gave me some aspirins when I went down to the kitchen."

Matt was surprised by the disappointment in Buck's expression.

"That's all, huh?"

Matt nodded. "That's it."

"You don't think she's pretty?"

Matt's gaze wandered over Buck's shoulder to the woman sitting gracefully in the saddle. It wasn't the first time he'd noticed what a terrific body was hidden under that royal blue T-shirt and snugly fitting jeans. He'd felt those firm, full breasts pressed against him, however briefly, last night and his hand had spread halfway around that slender waist. And those long legs . . . they could wrap around a man and guide him through his paces just as they were now gripping Stormy's sleek sides and keeping her under control.

And he certainly couldn't find fault with her face. Deceptively angelic with its small, pointed chin and oversize baby-blue eyes, he knew that beautiful face hid the soul of a barbarian. Had that spun-gold mass of hair been on any other woman, he would already have felt it sweep across his bare skin during the rhythmic motions of lovemaking.

He watched as she leaned forward, stretching her hand up Stormy's thick neck to adjust the strap. Matt felt his own body react instinctively to the sight of her T-shirt pulling taut over her breasts, highlighting the small, round nipples that thrust against the thin fabric. Yes, the week was just beginning. He would have her in his bed begging for more before he left next Friday.

Matt had the grace to flush slightly as he returned his attention to her father. Forcing a noncommittal tone, he answered, "She's not really my type. I guess she's not bad looking, but she sure has a temper."

"Dang it, I told her to act more like a lady. No man will ever want to share a blanket with her for the rest of his life. She's like a green-broke filly, tame enough to eat sugar out of your hand, but wild enough to bite a finger off in the process.''

Matt had felt the sting of her fury and the jagged edge of her revenge. He certainly couldn't disagree with her father's assessment of Jamie's rather unpleasant prospects, so he offered what little hope he could. "I wouldn't worry if I were you. I've heard the percentage of men to women out here in the West is so high that even the plainest woman has an excellent chance of finding a husband. If a man has a pair of spurs and a bullwhip, he should be able to handle your daughter.''

Buck's permanently squinted eyes drew even smaller as he studied Matt. Obviously deciding Matt was making a joke, Buck gave a hoarse chuckle and spit a stream of tobacco out the side of his mouth. "You might be right, son.''

"Now that you've divided into two groups, I want all the beginning riders to follow Boots over to those horses,'' Jamie announced, indicating a hitching post lined with horses as she wrapped up her speech. "And all the experienced riders should wait here, while I go into the barn and get your mounts.''

Matt glanced around and saw he'd been included in the "experienced" group. For a moment he considered telling her that he'd never touched a horse in his whole life, but as he watched her urge Stormy toward the barn, then dismount in one fluid motion, he decided it didn't look so difficult. After all, he could drive a powerful sports car and sail a yacht. How different could it be to sit on a saddle and steer a horse?

He wished he could have heard all those important instructions Jamie had given the rest of the guests, but Buck's interrogation had kept him distracted.

Oh well, he was a quick learner. And this was one more weakness he dared not let her discover. Heaven only knew what sort of pleasure she would get out of that.

One by one, Jamie brought out horses and matched them with riders. Matt watched closely as each person gathered the reins, stepped into a stirrup and swung into the saddle. Finally, everyone was sitting on a horse but him. Jamie went into the barn one last time and led out a stocky reddish-brown horse. Muscles rippled beneath his shiny coat and his eyes rolled suspiciously as he looked around at the other horses and people.

"I saved this one for you," Jamie said as she handed Matt the reins. "I figured you'd want a horse with a little spunk."

"I like my women spirited and my horses obedient," Matt told her, meeting her gaze with a lazy grin. "Or is that the other way around?"

"I think you like your women brainless and flat on their backs," Jamie commented, keeping her voice low enough so only he could hear her. She lifted her chin in that defiant gesture he was coming to know so well. "You might as well make friends with your horse," she continued. "That's the only thing you'll be kissing good-night around here."

Matt reached out to pat the horse's neck, but abruptly drew back when the horse's skin quivered under his hand. The horse twisted his head around, and man and beast eyed each other warily.

"I don't think he likes me," Matt commented.

"Horses are usually pretty good judges of character."

Matt glanced over his shoulder at Jamie. "You know what you need?"

She seemed a little taken back at his unexpected change of subject. "I need a lot of things, Mr. Montana. But I have a feeling you're not talking about money in the bank or good health."

"Those things are important, but what I think you need more than anything right now is some great sex."

Her eyes widened, but she retained her composure. "And I suppose you know someone who could provide that."

He tried for modesty, but failed. "I've put smiles on a few women's faces in my time."

Jamie threw up her hands, startling the horse and causing him to jerk his head up, pulling the reins out of Matt's hand. "You're incredible...and I don't mean that as a compliment. I've heard there were men in this world like you. But until yesterday I'd been lucky enough not to actually meet any." She whirled around and stalked toward her own horse.

Matt grabbed for the reins and held them at arm's length while the nervous horse snorted and glared at him with unfriendly eyes. "Settle down horse. You and I have got to get along for the next few days."

The horse didn't make any promises, but at least he didn't pull away as Matt separated the two reins and wrapped them over the saddle horn.

Copying what he'd seen the others do and what he'd described dozens of times in his book, Matt gripped the saddle horn and slipped his boot into the stirrup.

Just as he was pushing off the ground in an attempt to swing smoothly into the saddle, the horse sidled away.

Matt was left with no choice but to hop along on one foot while trying to catch up to the moving horse.

"Whoa dammit," he muttered as he frantically pulled back on the reins. The horse finally stopped and Matt again made an attempt to mount.

"Don't move or I swear I'll buy you and haul you straight to the glue factory."

The horse turned his head to watch the man. Matt was in midair, his leg lifted, when the horse decided to help. He thrust his nose between Matt's legs and tossed his head.

The effect was very much like a catapult as Matt reacted to the unexpected intimacy by overshooting the saddle. Only his left foot firmly anchored in the stirrup kept him from going all the way off the other side.

Hoping no one was watching, Matt pulled himself upright and settled on the saddle. The seat was slippery and the ground looked like it was miles below him, which didn't help his sagging confidence level. First he had to put up with a frustrated woman whose sharp tongue and knockout body were guaranteed to drive him crazy, and now he was stuck with the horse from hell.

The other riders were filing out of the corral, anxious to get acquainted with their horses in the larger open space of the pasture. Jamie was sitting astride Stormy, holding the gate open while the riders passed through.

Matt waited until everyone else had left the corral before he dug his heels into his horse's ribs. The animal leapt forward, almost unseating his rider with the speed of his response. Matt's automatic reaction was to jerk back on the reins. Again the horse obeyed, stopping so quickly that Matt almost vaulted over the animal's neck.

"Weren't you listening to my speech? Our horses come fully equipped with power steering and power brakes," Jamie remarked as she rode alongside of him. "Watch out or you'll go through the windshield."

"Where are the seat belts?" Matt straightened in the saddle and tried to look as if he was in complete control. "Just like a sports car, each horse handles a little differently. This horse and I'll be used to each other in no time." More cautiously he nudged the horse's sides and braced himself for the launch. Instead, the animal began walking forward as sedately as a hack horse.

He dared not tempt fate, so he didn't stop the horse and wait for Jamie while she shut the gate behind them. But she quickly caught up with him.

"Are you sure you know how to ride, Mr. Montana?"

"I'll admit I don't ride often," he answered in a major understatement. "Chicago isn't exactly the equine capital of the world."

She gave him another look that said she wasn't completely convinced of his equestrian skill, but she didn't pursue the issue.

"By the way," he said, deftly changing the subject. "Call me Matt." He flashed her a confident smile now that he felt a little more in control of the animal below him.

Jamie answered with a smile of her own, which should have made him instantly suspicious. Rising slightly in her stirrups, she clicked her tongue.

The horses responded immediately, picking up the pace to a bone-jarring trot. Parts of Matt's anatomy that he usually tried very hard to protect were being bruised against the hard seat as he bounced around. Finally, taking a cue from Jamie, he stood in the stirrups and let his knees absorb the shock while his rear stayed a safe distance away from the saddle.

"So that's what the pioneers used for birth control," he muttered, hoping this would be a short ride. If he wasn't careful, by the end of the week, he could be a soprano.

"What?" Jamie called.

"Uh...I was just wondering what my horse's name is."

There was an evil twinkle in her eye as she answered, "Terminator." She kicked her horse in the ribs and galloped off to join the others.

Matt nodded. "Perfect. Just perfect. If the altitude doesn't kill me, the horse will. This never happens to Duke King."

Chapter Five

Bullets whistled past his head and bit into the weathered wood of the barn behind him. He ducked behind the watering trough and waited for a break in the fire before he leveled his pistol at a bandido and pulled the trigger. His supply of ammunition was running dangerously low, so he had to make every shot count.

The bullet found its mark, and the bandido tumbled over the railing of the balcony and thudded limply onto the boardwalk. That lowered their number to six against one... and those were odds Duke could handle.

He pushed the last five bullets out of the small leather loops on his ammo belt. That meant he'd be one bullet short.

Another shower of bullets buried into the wall and the trough. Duke shoved his last rounds into the cylinder, pulled back the hammer and fired, taking down another robber.

He couldn't feel sorry for the men dodging behind cover across the street. Ever since Dry Gulch had hired him to be their temporary sheriff, he'd made it clear he would tolerate no thievery or murder. He could *understand how men sometimes got a little rowdy, drinking too much, gambling too heavily, going too long without a woman. He could overlook high spirits…hell, he'd be right over in that saloon with the rest of them if it weren't for these damn drifters who thought they could just ride into town and make a major, and completely unauthorized, withdrawal of all the payroll from the bank.*

They'd left him no option but to convince them that breaking the law in Dry Gulch was a fatal mistake.

Duke saw a motion out of the corner of his eye and reacted instinctively. His gun blasted, lowering the number to four, and a quick shot at a man on the roof behind him decreased it to three.

He took cover behind the trough again as the men sent a spray of protective gunfire while they repositioned themselves. But he caught one trying to make a dash to his horse and reduced the number to two.

Two men and only one bullet.

As if sensing he was vulnerable, the two remaining bandits became bolder. While one sent a barrage of gunfire that effectively kept Duke's head down, the other sneaked around to a more strategic vantage point.

His boot scraped on the ledge and Duke shot instinctively. His bullet found its mark, but the robber was able to get a shot off before he died.

The bullet hit Duke in the thigh. Luckily, it missed his bone and exited out the back side of his leg. He looked down at the wound and the widening puddle of blood soaking across his pants leg and dripping on the loose sand beneath him.

Another round of bullets reminded him there was one bandit left. One bandit with a gun and plenty of ammunition.

Duke jerked the bandanna from around his neck and tied a tourniquet around his leg. He would deal with the wound later. But right now he had to find a bullet.

There was a noise behind him and Duke whirled around, automatically pulling the trigger. The hammer clicked loudly against the empty cylinder.

"So, gringo," the outlaw said, his mouth twisting into a yellow-toothed grin beneath his long, dirty mustache. "You're out of bullets. If I believed in fair play, I'd give you one of mine and we could have a shoot-out in the street." He raised his pistol until its barrel was looking Duke dead between the eyes. Slowly his thumb pulled back the hammer. "Unfortunately for you, I have a reputation for being the meanest, sneakiest, nastiest SOB ever to cross the Rio Grande. And it's a reputation I'm damned proud of."

"Not even a low-down thief like you would shoot a man who's sitting on the ground," Duke reasoned. "You don't want being a coward added to your reputation."

The bandit considered Duke's words, then slowly lowered his pistol. "Okay, I'll let you stand. Then I'll shoot you."

Duke's mind churned, trying to come up with a way to shoot the outlaw before the outlaw shot him. Duke took his hat off and wiped his sweaty forehead on his sleeve. A flash of sunlight reflected on something in the hatband and Duke's gaze fell on his lucky bullet. It had been stuck in the hat band for so long, he'd *forgotten about it. But now was the time to test its powers.*

Bracing himself against the trough so he could stand, Duke shoved the bullet into the cylinder of his gun. Pivoting so quickly he caught the bandido by surprise, Duke pulled back the hammer and pointed it at the man's chest.

"You were wrong," Duke informed the man in a calm, confident voice. "I have one bullet left and it has your name on it."

The man's eyes widened as he found himself on the wrong end of a gun. "You're bluffing."

"I'll admit that I've done a little bluffing in my time." Duke's finger hovered over the trigger. "But I guarantee that, right this minute, I do have a bullet in this gun. Now I want you to drop your revolver and raise your hands."

The bandit hesitated, apparently weighing his chances of beating Duke. Then, with a confident but foolish laugh, he raised his gun.

Duke's finger tightened and his lucky bullet proved its worth. Slowly the outlaw's fingers opened and the pistol slid out of his hand and dropped onto the sand. His black eyes glazed, but continued staring at Duke even as he melted limply onto the sand at Duke's feet.

With the toe of his boot, Duke flipped the robber onto his back. As if the dead man could hear him, Duke said, "You picked the wrong town, Mister... and the wrong guy. Nobody crosses Duke King and lives."

The townspeople rushed out from their hiding places.

"That was the best shooting I've ever seen."

"Thanks, Sheriff. You saved our town."

"Look, he's bleeding."

Duke barely glanced down at the sticky stain still spreading down his leg. "It's nothing."

A young boy looked at the bloody wound and reached up to tug on Duke's shirtsleeve. "But Mr. King, don't it hurt?"

Duke reached down and tousled the boy's hair. "Of course it don't hurt, son. I'm a man."

"What trash!"

The book flew across the room and settled against the wall in the same spot as before. If Darlene hadn't picked it up and put it on Jamie's nightstand, she never would have been tempted to open it again.

What an inexcusable waste of trees! How could these books have become bestsellers? *I'm a man.* What kind of stupid boast was that?

But then, the more she got to know Matt Montana, the easier it was to see where he'd gotten the characterization for Duke King. They were two sides of the same coin and neither had a clue what a *real* man was.

And Matt seemed determined to prove his manliness in all the wrong ways, for all the wrong reasons.

Who did he think he was fooling? If he had ever sat on a horse before, Jamie would eat her saddle blanket. Sooner or later his masculine pride was going to get him into trouble.

Jamie suspected it would be sooner.

When she'd seen him slipping and sliding across the smooth leather seat of the saddle, she should have confronted him right then and there. But a mischievous streak had convinced her he deserved everything he got. If he wanted to push his way onto the ranch and lie about his abilities, he was an adult and he could suffer the consequences of his oversize ego.

He was the most annoying man she'd ever met.

And, although she hated the weakness of character it showed, she'd never been more sexually attracted to any other human.

She didn't know what it was about him, but there was raw, rugged masculinity that was incredibly sensual. He was all rough edges and phony bravado, but the twinkle in those surprisingly blue eyes and the perfection of that incredible body was enough to melt the strongest resolve.

Maybe she was being a little too rough on him. Maybe he wasn't as obnoxious as he seemed. But Jamie's defense mechanism had already kicked in, a defense meant to protect her heart from being broken and her body from being used by a weekend cowboy she'd never see again. She'd had a very brief affair with a lawyer from Atlanta two years ago. When he left, returning to a wife Jamie hadn't known he had and a life that definitely didn't include a gullible cowgirl from Colorado, she'd learned a painful but valuable lesson.

And the thing that frightened her most was that she was a hundred times more attracted to Matt than she'd ever been to that jerk from Atlanta. Attracted, but repulsed. She had no idea how that was possible, but with Matt Montana, a modern-day Casanova and the creator of Duke King, a historical Casanova, he'd made an art out of inspiring strong feelings.

JAMIE LED a predawn trail ride for those hearty souls who wanted to watch the sun rise over the Rockies. As she expected, there were only about a dozen people who could rouse themselves out of their comfortable beds for the chilly early-morning ride, and Matt wasn't one of them.

She intentionally kept the difficulty of the ride to a novice level because many of the riders were children and the first half of the ride was in almost total darkness.

They arrived at the top of the small hill just as the eastern sky was beginning to lighten. Everyone dismounted, practiced tying their horses to trees or low limbs, then wrapped themselves, or in the case of the newlyweds and some of the families, small groups of two or three, with the blankets they had brought. They followed Jamie's lead as she found a smooth boulder to serve as a back brace and sat on the rocky knoll, waiting for God to create an aerial masterpiece.

Shades of darkest rose and palest mauve began sending out tentative streaks across the almost colorless gray sky. Gradually growing more bold, the light inched upward and outward until it chased away the last traces of the night's gloom. At the last few moments before the sun actually put in an appearance, the jagged mountain peaks, especially the ones with the snowcaps, absorbed all the colors of the sky and glowed like a mythical Camelot.

People spoke in awed whispers, as if talking aloud would break the spell. Jamie smiled, pleased that the sight was being properly appreciated. She had grown up seeing the special beauty of western Colorado every day. . . and she planned on being surrounded by it for the rest of her life.

But now that Hollywood had discovered the area, they weren't making her resolve easy. Several movies had already been filmed on nearby ranches, and Jamie couldn't object to that too much. Not only did it give a dramatic boost to the local economy, but all of the movies, so far, had picked up on the very best points of the landscape and captured the flavor of the lifestyle. However, that talent had brought about the other, more damaging Hollywood element—the absentee landlord.

Jamie thought of them as nouveau riche sharks, gobbling up anything that struck their fancy. Several ranches had already been sold, the latest to a very famous talk show hostess who would probably turn the place into a showplace for what she considered Western chic, but which, in reality, couldn't be further from authentic. Security gates would take the place of the rustic cedar rails, and the roads would be widened and paved to allow a smoother ride for their Mercedes and Porsches. It would be the death of the real West.

And yet Jamie could understand why her neighbors were selling out. The money being offered was almost obscene, and with the economy at an all-time low and the cost of living at an all-time high, it was easy to see why the ranchers were taking the cash and moving away.

But that wouldn't happen to the Rocky K if Jamie had anything to say about it. How tragic to think her children might be able to sit on the top of a hill and watch a glorious sunrise over the mountains only when they were on vacation. The world would be a better place if everyone could start their day looking at such a glorious sunrise as she and her guests had just witnessed.

When the sun finished its climb over the peaks, the sky began taking on the pure, clear blue that was so typical of a summer day. Jamie helped everyone mount and reorganized the trail ride for the trip back to the ranch, where a hearty breakfast would be waiting.

Now that all the guests had checked in, the meals were served in a large building that had been dubbed the Mess Hall. Besides providing the space for enough tables to seat all the guests, there was a wood plank floor that, once the tables and chairs were pushed against the walls, provided a great place for dancing. A much larger building stood nearby that was used to exercise horses in the winter and to host local gatherings such as rodeos and stock shows.

Boots and Darlene worked together, tolerating each other long enough to prepare the meals in the well-equipped commercial-size kitchen.

Jamie made a point of sitting with different groups of guests at every meal, getting to know them better and paying attention to their comments and suggestions. Her father, too, seemed to enjoy the communal meals because it gave him a constantly changing audience for his tales of the wild West. But ever since Matt Montana had arrived on the scene, Buck hadn't spent much time with the other guests. He was, for very different reasons than his daughter, totally fascinated by the man. It was evident Buck saw none of Matt's flaws... flaws that were glaringly obvious to Jamie.

Jamie noted with wry amusement that although Matt hadn't made it out of bed in time for the trail ride, he'd apparently made a point of not missing breakfast again. She was less amused when he carried his tray to her table and sat across from her. She could tell by the way he eased down on the wooden chair that the brief ride yesterday had taken its toll on his muscles.

"So what's on the agenda for today?" he asked while buttering three steaming biscuits.

"Well, you've already missed a trail ride."

"I'm not a morning person," he commented. "Give me a sunset over a sunrise any day. Besides, it's not really a *manly* thing to sit around admiring scenery."

Jamie was reminded of the passage she had read last night. "Yes, and you're big on being a *man,* aren't you?"

He seemed a little bewildered by her question. "Of course I am. It sort of goes with the gender. Men have more important things on their minds than sunrises and mountain views."

"Thank goodness the men who settled the West didn't feel that way or they'd all have stayed in Kansas."

The guest on her right asked her a question, and Jamie was grateful for the opportunity to turn her attention away from Matt. She was glad he hadn't gone on the trail ride this morning. If he'd spoken one word of criticism during that spectacular sunrise, she would probably have ruined the moment by punching him square in that handsome face.

When most of the guests had finished their meals, Jamie stood and announced, "We have a chapel for anyone who wants to worship privately on this Sunday morning. There will be wranglers in the corral area all day in case you should want to get better acquainted with your horse *and* your saddle. But please confine your rides to the small pasture north of the barn. We'll also be organizing some volleyball games and a horseshoe tournament after lunch, and the pool will be open all afternoon. Then, tonight we'll have our big Happy Trails barbecue followed by a barn dance right here in the mess hall.''

A murmur of excitement rose from the crowd, and Jamie had to wait for the noise to die down so she could add, "And tomorrow morning, our Western adventures begin."

She was able to give Matt a genuine smile because she knew that tomorrow she and he would go their separate ways for the next five days. Jamie would be riding with the wagon train which all but four of the guests had requested. Those four, including three male schoolteachers from New Jersey and Matt, had signed up for a mountain trail ride that would wind deep into the Uncompahgre National Forest, climbing to the top of the San Juan mountain range and following the rugged peaks, not returning until next Friday. And the best part about that trip would be that her father would be leading it, with Boots along as the cook and wrangler.

She and Matt reached the door at the same time. He stopped and indicated that she should go ahead. But as a host giving deference to a guest, she paused and motioned for him to pass through first. One corner of his sensual mouth lifted in a smile that was more teasing than amused as he walked out the door.

As a host, she should have felt nothing. However, as a woman, she felt insulted. He could have put up at least a token argument. When he waited for her, she would have walked right by, but his long strides easily kept up with her.

She tried to keep the pettiness out of her voice as she told him, "You should do a little riding this afternoon. The trail you'll be on is rough, and it would help if you were a little more comfortable in the saddle."

Instantly she saw his defenses rise. Even though he was obviously sore, he was determined to hide his unfamiliarity with a saddle. "I'm just fine on horseback. And I'm in good shape. That ride should be a piece of cake."

It was Jamie's turn to give him a crooked grin. She would enjoy watching him eat those words.

So FAR his "Western experience" hadn't done anything to help his writer's block. But it was doing wonders for his ego.

The word had spread among all the guests, and even those who weren't fans of Western literature made it a point to stop and ask for his autograph or to tell him how much they admired anyone who could write books. And then there were, as in any crowd, a couple of people who thought their own life story would make a fascinating novel and proceeded to tell him all the boring details.

But the time he enjoyed most was spent with Buck as they sat on lawn chairs by the pool, discussing real history as compared to the history portrayed in fiction and in the movies.

It was odd how well Matt and Buck got along considering their very different backgrounds and lifestyles. In fact, Matt seldom bonded with other people because he preferred being alone to allowing someone else to dictate where he would go, what he would do and when he would do it. Friends were an added responsibility. Matt didn't have time to nourish a friendship, especially because it would take away some of the control he had on his life. And control was one of the things Matt valued most.

That was why this writing problem was driving him crazy. It was ruining his career, a career he had carefully planned and developed. If he couldn't regain control of his creativity...well, he didn't want to think about that possibility. After all, that was why he was here, in Nowhere, Colorado, spending time with a horse who wanted him dead and a woman who wanted him deader. He would put up with anything to get back the enthusiasm and imagination that fueled his writing. Anything! Even Jamie Kimball and her evil twin, Terminator.

She was probably really enjoying that little joke. Of all the horses west of the Mississippi, she had chosen one with an attitude. While the other guests trotted and turned their animals like old pros, Matt was dreading the minute he'd feel that hard saddle under his rear again. Hadn't these people heard of padded seats?

But then, she was probably getting a laugh out of that, too. Well, he'd show her he was tough. By the time he got back from that trail ride, he'd be riding like the Lone Ranger.

"Hey, Matt, come join the game," a guy named Lyle called. "We need another player. The other team's slaughtering us."

Matt glanced at Buck and hesitated. But Buck nodded his encouragement.

"Go on, son," Buck said. "We'll have plenty of time to talk on the trail."

Matt pulled his T-shirt off and tossed it on the chair before joining Lyle's team. He looked through the net, assessing his opponents, but his gaze got no farther than Jamie's long, shapely legs, most of which were exposed by a pair of very short cut-offs. Their frayed hems barely covered her rounded cheeks...and he definitely didn't mean the ones on her face. As she leapt, arms raised, her back toward him as she set up the ball for a spike, the shorts hiked up to a dangerous height. His attention strayed from the ball as his eyes strained to see more of the untanned skin that was being revealed.

Suddenly an explosion of white stars danced across his vision. He staggered, then was knocked aside as someone volleyed the ball that had just been slammed against his head and bounced straight up into the air.

"Good save," Lyle said, patting Matt on the back as the play continued.

Yeah, good save, Matt thought woozily. At least he knew where they kept the aspirins.

The other team rotated and Jamie moved into the position directly across the net from Matt. Her hair, as usual, was pulled back into a ponytail, but long, golden tendrils had slipped loose and were blowing across her face. She brushed them back with her hands and met his gaze with those wide, very blue eyes that somehow managed to look so innocent even with that knowing, devilish twinkle dancing in them. It told him that she knew exactly what he'd been looking at, and that she thought he'd gotten just what he deserved.

Matt forced his attention back to the volleyball game. That woman would be the death of him yet. The score was now two to three, and he was losing.

Chapter Six

The room was filled with bright colors, laughter and the tangy smell of barbecue.

Matt took his place in line at a long buffet table that held heaping platters of barbecued ribs, chicken and brisket, along with huge bowls of potato salad, baked beans, coleslaw and plates piled with corn on the cob. A group of local ranchers provided the music and began tuning their fiddles and basses as the guests lined up for dinner. By the time the last piece of chocolate cake disappeared and all the homemade ice cream was gone, everyone was ready to dance.

Matt's experience on the dance floor didn't include the Texas two-step or the Cotton-eye Joe. He watched while Jamie selected one of the male guests and demonstrated the steps. She and her partner made it look so simple that all the guests from the youngest to the oldest were soon circling the room, more or less following the appropriate patterns.

The fact that it didn't matter if someone missed a step or even if they made up some new ones of their own, made the event more fun. Matt was hesitant at first, standing back and watching until Buck grabbed

Matt's arm and pulled him into the middle of the semiorganized chaos.

"Come on, son," Buck shouted over the noise of the lively music and dozens of feet stomping on the wooden floor. "This is how *real* cowboys dance. Consider this research."

Matt sincerely doubted he would ever be able to use either of the dances in his books, but everyone looked like they were having so much fun, he joined in. Somehow he became partnered with a teenage girl who was delighted to guide him through the paces. So delighted that she danced a little too close and rubbed her young, but well-developed body against him with a little too much enthusiasm.

Over the girl's shoulder, Matt intercepted a disapproving look from Jamie. He lifted his hands, palms up in a helpless gesture. She rolled her eyes and shook her head as if it was all his fault.

Her partner whirled her away, and Matt lost sight of her for several minutes. He did manage to change his own partner to what he thought would be a safer, less aggressive lady. But when the middle-aged woman pinched his butt and offered him her cabin key, Matt began wondering if it could, somehow, truly be his fault. Was he sending out some sort of mental message? Was his sexuality more potent out here in the West?

Or maybe it was the clothes. Only his jeans and his underwear weren't brand new. He glanced down at the gray ostrich-skin boots that were squeezing all the life out of his feet and reached up to touch the black Stetson hat he'd purchased at a Western clothing store in Chicago. Over a blue-striped cowboy shirt, complete with pearlized buttons, he wore a black leather vest. It wasn't his usual choice of outfit, but it was sort of fun for a change.

And if women went for it in such a big way, maybe he'd have to try wearing his cowboy duds back in Chicago.

He brushed off his current partner's proposition with a refusal so charming that she was still smiling when he left her at the punch bowl.

Matt checked out the refreshments and was disappointed not to find anything stronger than fruit punch. That was one of the drawbacks of a family-focused organization. Thank God there wouldn't be any children on his trail ride. There would be no one along to whine about the conditions or slow them down. Everyone would be strong and tough, as rugged as the mountains around them. Everyone would be men. *Thank God,* he repeated.

A flash of red caught his attention, and he let his gaze focus on Jamie as she danced by with yet another partner. Her silky blond hair was spilling in a loose, rippling cascade down over her shoulder as she leaned her head back to laugh at something the guy had said.

Why didn't she ever laugh like that when he was around? She was one woman who didn't seem to find any appeal in his Western attire or anything else about him.

But beneath that standoffish attitude, he sensed she wasn't quite as indifferent to him as she tried to imply. He'd intercepted looks when she hadn't had her guard up. They had been speculative, as if she was imagining how good they could be together.

A new guy cut in, immediately pulling Jamie into his arms in a much tighter embrace than any of her other partners. Instead of taking his hands, she looped her arms around his neck.

Matt shifted, trying to keep her in sight as she circled the dance floor. Who was that guy, anyway? Matt didn't remember seeing him at any of the ranch activities, so he probably wasn't a guest. Jamie's boyfriend, perhaps? For no logical reason, that thought annoyed him. She hadn't mentioned a boyfriend. Not that he and she had had many civil, personal conversations. A boyfriend could complicate Matt's plans for Jamie . . . plans that would make his visit to the Rocky K Ranch a little more pleasurable.

They danced past again, with the strange man holding her hands over her head and twirling her in circles. Her long hair whipped across her face while her full, layered skirt swirled around her legs. Then, as the song ended, he bent her backward in a dramatic dip.

Her hair swept along the floor, so close to Matt that it brushed against his boots. Her red ruffled peasant blouse barely held in the fullness of her breasts as they threatened to spill out of the low neckline in her inverted position. Her cheeks were flushed and her lips were open in a delighted smile. For an instant her eyes met his, then her partner pulled her upright. She turned her back to Matt and joined the rest of the guests as they clapped for the band.

Matt decided he'd had enough. He threaded his way through the crowd and out the front door. Another smaller, but even noisier group was standing around a mechanical bull, cheering on a rider. As Matt watched, the man lost his balance and tumbled off onto the thick cushion of hay that surrounded the leather-covered machine.

Buck noticed Matt and immediately came over to stand next to him.

"You next?" he asked Matt.

Matt tried not to let his expression reflect his true feelings. He couldn't think of anyone or anything that would get him up on that electric monster. Terminator was enough excitement for him.

"Nah, it looks like there's a long line," he hedged, not wanting Buck to know the truth. "I think I'll just head off to bed."

Buck leaned closer and whispered, "There's a few cans of *special punch* in that ice chest around the corner. Jamie'd have my hide if she knew about it."

Matt wasn't much of a drinker, but tonight it suited his mood. He and Buck slipped around the corner of the mess hall into the semidarkness. Buck slushed around in the ice chest until he pulled out two ice-cold cans of beer.

"Here's one for now and one to take with you," he said, handing both to Matt. "Help yourself if you want more."

"Thanks." Matt pulled the tab and held the can out as some of the foam bubbled out. He downed most of the contents of the can in one swallow.

Buck gave him a curious look. "Woman trouble?"

"Ha, I should be so lucky." Matt finished off the beer and crushed the can in his hand.

"We don't have any single females your age in this group. But I'm sure there's one or two local girls you might be interested in getting to know a little better."

He nudged Matt companionably. "If you know what I mean."

Matt shifted, uncomfortable with the direction the conversation was taking. He knew exactly what Buck meant, but Buck didn't realize it was his own daughter who had caught Matt's fancy. "Uh . . . I think I'll head over to the barn and say good-night to my horse." Say good-night to his horse? Where had that come from? Matt opened the other can and said, "Night, Buck. See you bright and early in the morning."

He leaned against the corral rails and sipped the cold drink while he stared off into the distance. A sliver of crescent moon had just risen over the mountains, making them look even bigger and more rugged in silhouette. It wasn't the moon that lit the sky, but the billions of stars glowing brightly from horizon to horizon.

He'd known things would be different here than they were in the city, but he hadn't expected such extremes. The darkness was so thick and black, he could, for the first time, imagine the depth of the universe. The city lights washed out the night and made the sky seem flat and cold. He'd never noticed the dimensional layers of stars or how they seemed to be alive, with individual personalities. He'd studied astronomy and knew stars were different colors, but he'd only seen them as distant white dots rather than the sparkling blue and red jewels they appeared to be in this sky.

And the silence of the night was so intense that even the small sounds were magnified, but separated so that each could be heard distinctly. Even as the music from the dance hung in the still night air, Matt could clearly hear the chirp of crickets and the patter of moths flying against the light bulbs inside the barn.

The sound of a footstep on the hard-packed dirt was like thunder in his ears. Matt looked toward the noise and saw Jamie walking though the wide, open doorway into the barn. And she was alone.

Matt drained the can in a final swallow and tossed it in a metal barrel that was used as a garbage can. The alcohol, combined with the altitude, made him lightheaded, and perhaps a little short on the ability to think clearly.

Walking with an unsteady swagger, he followed Jamie. She was standing in front of a stall, stroking Stormy's dappled nose. She barely glanced in his direction as he approached her.

"Your absence was noticed," she commented.

"By you?" he asked, not stopping until he was directly behind her, so close he could smell the sweet fragrance of her hair.

"Of course not," she snorted. "I didn't even realize you'd left until a half dozen of my female guests asked me where you were. They were all hoping for a dance—" she slid him a suggestive arch of her eyebrows "—or something."

His hands spanned her waist and he whirled her around so quickly that she didn't have time to resist. "I was hoping it was you who wanted to dance . . . or something with me," he murmured, then leaned over and covered her lips with his.

They were soft and sweet just as he'd guessed they would be. Her mouth opened in a gasp of surprise and she stiffened in his grasp, but Matt didn't stop. The tip of his tongue traced around the inside curve of her lips, teasing, caressing, pulling a response from her. He felt the whisper of her sigh against his mouth. For an instant she answered his kiss with a raw passion that matched his own. His body reacted quickly, pressing hotly against the barrier of his jeans. Needing to feel her flesh rub against him, he took a step closer, backing her against the door of the stall.

His hand stroked upward from her waist until his fingers brushed against the underside of one firm breast. He was pleasantly surprised to discover she wasn't wearing a bra. The hardness of her nipples pushed against his chest and he became obsessed with the desire to touch her, to feel the warmth of her skin. His kisses became more demanding as his hand slipped inside the low, elastic neckline of her blouse and cupped her breast in his palm. She wasn't large, but she filled his hand with pure perfection. The ache in his groin grew increasingly urgent.

Suddenly, all the air in his lungs exhaled in a shocked groan as her fist landed in the pit of his stomach with stunning force.

"Why'd you do that?" he gasped, struggling to catch his breath.

Jamie adjusted her blouse, tucking the tempting swell of her breast out of sight. "It was either a punch in the gut or a knee in the groin."

"Bad choices," he groaned. "What happened to a gentle slap?"

"I know that your hero, Dude King, thinks a gentle slap is foreplay. And I have a feeling there's a lot of you in your character."

"It's *Duke*," he gasped, then looked up at her from his bent position as he still clasped his hands across his stomach. "You've read my books?" He was inordinately pleased that she was discussing the elements of his novels, even though he knew she hadn't meant the reference to be flattering to either him or Duke.

"I don't care for that kind of literature," she answered. "It's too sexist and unromantic for my taste, but I've flipped through one of them. *Bandido of Dry Gulch,* I think."

His author's ego staggered under her verbal blow that was even more painful than her fist. "It's *Desperado of Dry Gulch,* not Bandido," he corrected.

"Desperado, bandido, what's the difference?"

Slowly he straightened as his lungs recovered. "Well...not much by definition. But I see them as having very different motivations. A bandido is an outlaw by choice...a desperado is trying to run away, but his past keeps catching up with him."

"Whatever...but my point is that you, like your characters, don't know how to take no for an answer."

"I never heard a *no*."

"You never heard a 'yes'."

He looked directly into her eyes, compelling her not to turn away. "You wanted that kiss as much as I did. I could *feel* it whenever I was around you. I could *see* it in your eyes. You wanted it, then you didn't know what to do with it."

"I did *not* want you to kiss me."

"Did, too."

"Not."

"Too."

They faced off, glaring at each other, their earlier emotions replaced by a different, but equally strong passion.

"I'm not part of the package, buster. The activities listed in the brochure do not include sex with the personnel."

"Damn, and I thought I saw Darlene wink at me earlier," he retorted with a wry smile.

The long, dark fringe of her eyelashes dropped across her eyes, momentarily hiding her expression. But when she looked back at him, her eyes were burning as hotly as the stars in the heavens. "Your macho ego is out of control if you think every woman is just panting over you, waiting breathlessly for you to overpower her with your charm. Well, here's a news flash for you. Your charm may work on some females, but it has absolutely no effect on me."

His gaze focused pointedly on the outline of her nipples that still thrust tautly against the cotton material of her blouse. "*No* effect?"

She crossed her arms over her chest. "None at all. Don't confuse the chill of the night with any sort of sexual response."

"You probably wouldn't recognize sexual attraction if it bit you on the..."

"Jamie, come quick," a voice outside the barn shouted. "Your father's been hurt."

All the anger drained from her face, replaced by fear. Without another word to Matt, she ran out of the barn.

He followed her to where most of the guests crowded in a circle, staring down at someone lying on the hay. The group parted, allowing Jamie through, and she knelt next to her father.

"Dad, what's wrong?" she asked. "Is it your heart?"

Her father looked up at her, his pained grin a little sheepish. "No, it's my gosh darn back. I think I pulled a muscle."

She leaned back on her heels. "How'd you do that? Were you dancing the lambada again?"

"Nah, nothing like that."

"Well?" she prompted, obviously not willing to let him avoid answering her question.

"Well...I guess you could say it happened when that dang bull bucked me off."

Jamie shook her head in disbelief. "You rode the bull?"

"Almost. And I had it up to top speed," he added, unable to resist boasting. "The buzzer went off right when I hit the hay."

"I'll get the van and take you to the doctor."

"Nah, I'll be fine. Everyone just go back to your dancing or whatever." He waited until the others began turning away, returning to the mess hall, then he motioned for Matt to kneel down. "Help me up. This is really embarrassing," he murmured.

"I don't know if we should move him," Jamie said doubtfully.

"Nothin's broken," Buck stated, growing more agitated by the minute. "Just get me to my bed."

Matt could have easily picked the older man up and carried him to the house. But he suspected Buck would be even more embarrassed to be treated like an invalid. So, he eased Buck to his feet, keeping a firm hold on him until he was able to stand upright.

Buck grimaced with each movement. "It's hell getting old," he muttered.

Jamie circled like a worried hen, trying to help, but Buck kept shooing her away. He took a few steps on his own, then accepted her arm on one side and Matt's arm on the other. Slowly they walked across the yard and into the house.

Matt waited outside the bathroom until Buck finished using the facilities. By the time they made it to the older man's bedroom, Jamie had found the heating pad and plugged it in. She left long enough for Buck to undress and crawl painfully into bed, then returned to tuck him in.

"I still think I should call the doctor."

"This happened a couple of years ago and all he told me was to stay in bed for a few days and get some rest." Buck's expression was stubborn as he pulled the blanket up to this chin. "I'm not going to pay that old quack to tell me what I already know."

"I've got to get back to the guests..." Jamie was heading for the door when she slid to a stop and turned back to Buck. Her eyes were wide and worried. "Tomorrow the trail rides begin. Who's going to take your place?"

"You can."

"No, I can't. I'm going to be leading the wagon train through the pass."

"Sam can handle that," Buck stated. "I'm sure he'd be glad to take care of the wagon train if you'd ask him nicely. But you *have* to lead the trail ride. No one knows those mountains as good as you do…except me, of course. I wouldn't trust our guests with anyone else."

Now it was Matt's turn to be alarmed. "She can't go with us."

"Why not?" Jamie and Buck asked simultaneously.

"Because she's a woman."

"So?" Jamie asked, her eyes beginning to shoot a fresh flurry of sparks. "What's your point?"

Matt sensed he was walking on dangerous ground, but he couldn't keep from voicing his objection. "This trail ride means a lot to me. It's more than just a fantasy cowboy thing like it is for the other guys. I *need* this experience. And I *need* it to be as realistic as possible."

"Jamie's a fine guide. She can tell you all about the history as you go."

"I don't want a history lesson. I want to *feel* the same things the frontiersmen felt and *see* the same things they saw. I'm sure your daughter is perfectly capable, but I don't think the trip'll have the right mood if she's along."

"Would you two quit talking about me as if I'm not here?"

Matt turned toward Jamie. "Look, don't take this personally. This has nothing to do with what happened in the barn."

"What happened in the barn?" Buck asked, looking expectantly from Jamie to Matt.

Matt ignored Buck and continued. "This ride is a male bonding kind of thing. It's going to be tough, and having a woman along will only slow us down. I'm sorry, but I just think it'll ruin the whole trip."

"Jamie's not *really* a woman," her father declared, successfully putting his foot in his mouth as he tried to mollify Matt. "She's just one of the boys."

She turned her fury on Buck. "I'll ignore that remark because you obviously landed on your head and aren't thinking clearly."

Buck snuggled deeper under the covers. "You're right. I need my rest. Jamie, you're just going to have to take over for me. And Matt, Jamie's tougher than you think. Give her a chance. If you're not pleased with the trip, I'll give you your money back."

Jamie stepped closer to Matt and whispered, "You want tough? You'll get tough."

Buck winced as he tried to find a more comfortable position. "Now get out of here, both of you, and let this old man get his rest. And you'd better get some sleep yourselves because sunrise will be here before you know it."

Jamie gave Matt one more disgusted glance, then looked back at her father. "I'm going to tell Darlene to take you to the doctor if you aren't feeling better in a couple of days. And Dad, don't drive her crazy. Good cooks are hard to find."

"I'm a perfect patient," Buck scoffed.

"Yeah, I know. I remember last winter when you had the flu. I was ready to drag you out in the snow and let you die."

"Is that any way for a daughter to talk about her father?" Buck pretended to be hurt. "It's a woman's duty to take care of her menfolk."

Jamie paused in the doorway and glanced over her shoulder. "I'm not a woman, remember. And this ol' boy is going to wrap up the festivities and go to bed."

Matt sighed, not at all happy with the turn of events, but accepting the fact that there was nothing he could do to change it. "Good night, Buck. I guess I'll be turning in, too."

"Good night, son. I'm sure you'll get everything you've been looking for on the trail ride."

"I hope so, sir." But he couldn't keep the disappointment from his voice.

"Oh, and Jamie," her father called, stopping her as she stepped into the hallway. "What *did* happen in the barn?"

Jamie gave Matt a steady look. "Nothing," she answered. "Absolutely nothing."

Chapter Seven

It was one o'clock before Jamie was able to break up the party. Then she spent another hour talking Sam into giving up a trip to San Francisco so he could play trail boss to a bunch of make-believe pioneers. The next hour was spent unpacking her wagon-train clothes and gear and packing much more compactly for the trail ride. She had to choose her clothes wisely, not only because of the drastic swings in temperature, but also because everything had to be packed into one duffle and two saddlebags.

Dawn came much too early for her. The alarm went off even before the rooster woke up. Jamie cursed the real estate market, the economy and the circumstances that were forcing her to get up at such an ungodly hour, after too little sleep, to begin a journey that would be both physically and emotionally exhausting.

She stopped by the mess hall long enough to make sure that Darlene and Boots had started breakfast. Then she rang the large bell that hung outside, waking up the guests who weren't already up and calling everyone for the meal. However, Jamie didn't have time to dawdle over bacon and eggs and had Darlene wrap a couple of biscuit and sausage sandwiches for her to eat later.

Sam drove up just as she reached the barn.

"You owe me a big one for this," Sam said as he dropped a kiss on her cheek. "I'm missing a conference on land development to help you out."

"Good! If I'd known you were going to San Francisco for that, I'd have thought of something sooner," Jamie responded.

He draped his arm around her shoulder. "I can think of quite a few things you could do to keep me home and happy."

"Yeah, we could play Monopoly and make fudge," she teased. This was a conversation she and Sam had had often while growing up. At one time it had been assumed they would marry and unite their families' ranches. But an attempt at serious dating proved she and Sam were better friends than lovers.

"I had something a little more meaningful in mind," he added, "such as polishing my boots and ironing my shirts."

She gave him a mock indignant look. "I muck stalls, clean toilets and laugh at jokes I've heard two hundred times. But I *never* iron."

"I forgot that you're the only person in Telluride High's history to flunk home economics."

Jamie shrugged with a total lack of remorse. "As I remember, your stuffed pillows won the sewing award that year. That's a skill that's sure to come in handy. I'll bet your father was pretty proud of that."

"Shh. You promised never to tell anyone about that."

"Good, then we're even." She handed him an arm-load of harness. "Be sure you protect my guests from Indian attacks. I don't want to lose any repeat customers." With a jaunty wave, she picked up a bucket of grooming tools and headed for the stalls where the horses were already eating their breakfast.

The wagon train got off on time, heading southwest from the ranch. They would keep to more level land while making a big loop, setting up a new camp each night and arriving back at the ranch on Friday.

But because Jamie was running back and forth between the wagons and saddling the trail horses, the trail ride left the ranch about an hour later than scheduled.

Instead of riding from the ranch, they loaded the horses and mules into trailers and the equipment and riders into trucks for the twenty-mile trip to the trailhead.

Along with Matt were the three teachers. None had much experience with horses, but all were eager to give it a try. And more important, as far as Jamie was concerned, they weren't upset at the sudden change of leadership. It made it easier to overlook Matt's bad attitude.

Jamie drove one truck, sharing the cab with Randy and Lyle while Boots drove the other one with Matt and Dale riding with him. They turned off the paved road near a town so small it had only one commercial business, a combination grocery and liquor store with a gas pump in front. As they wound their way through several private ranches, Jamie continued a conversation with her two passengers. Because she had been scheduled to lead the wagon train, she'd focused more on those guests. Now she was trying to become better acquainted with two of the men she would be spending twenty-four hours a day with for the next five days.

She discovered that all three teachers were married and taught at the same high school in Newark. Randy was a football coach who also taught a couple of classes of history and government, and Lyle specialized in all levels of math, while Dale, in the other truck, was a biology teacher. Jamie was glad they all were sensible, intelligent men who were used to following orders, because it would make her job easier. Everyone except Matt, who seemed determined not to cooperate.

By the time they reached the last private ranch before the national forest section began, it was almost noon. They parked the trucks a few feet off the dirt road near a clump of trees. Then while Jamie unloaded the horses and mules, Boots put together a quick lunch. It took careful planning and lots of practice to balance the load of all the tents, cooking equipment, food and other essential items on the two mules, leaving each rider to carry his or her own bedding and clothes tied behind their saddles.

"Okay everyone, listen up," Jamie said as they sat on their horses, ready to begin their adventure. "I don't want to frighten you by making this type of ride seem overly dangerous. But remember, we won't be in a controlled situation. This is not a pony ride in the park. We've tried to consider and plan for every possible problem, but something new always seems to happen.

"The first two days we'll be riding hard. The going will be rough, and it's vital that you remain alert at all times." She pointed to one of the shorter mountains in the sprawling range. "I know of a beautiful campsite by a lake near the summit, and we'll spend Tuesday and Wednesday nights there, then head back down."

Matt squinted up at the craggy peak she indicated. "You're not talking about that little one, are you?"

Jamie bit back a sharp reply. Instead, she forcibly modulated her tone as she replied, "Yes, that's the one."

He gave her a look that clearly said he was disappointed in the choice.

"It's bigger than it looks," Jamie commented. "Believe me, you'll wish it wasn't so steep by the time we get to the top. You'll be begging me to stop and let you rest."

"I don't beg for anything," he said

"We'll see." It was more of a challenge than a promise, and Matt accepted it with a cocky grin.

Jamie reined her horse around. "Most of the trails are wild animal paths, so they're narrow and not very well defined. Follow me, single file unless we're crossing an opening. Boots will bring up the rear."

She took the lead rope of Maybelline, one of the mules, from him and hitched it loosely to a ring behind her saddle. In case of emergency, it would release easily. Otherwise, it would help the mule to keep her mind on business rather than wandering off the trail or stopping for a snack. Mules worked hard, but never eagerly and had to be constantly kept to task.

They lived up to their reputation of being stubborn, single-minded and very self-centered.

Just like some people she knew. Jamie glanced back as Matt cut in behind Maybelline. Yes, certain people and mules had a lot in common.

Jamie pushed hard, keeping a steady pace through the first leg of their journey as she tried to make up for the time they'd lost. She wanted to get to a special spot near an alpine meadow before they made camp for the night.

The horses had to pick their way carefully over the uneven paths, trying to find solid ground beneath the loose rocks. Jamie demonstrated how to lean backward and keep a firm, but loose rein when going down a steep decline and how to lean forward when going up an incline. She cautioned about watching for low branches, then waited a half dozen times while the men went back to retrieve their hats when they forgot to duck.

"Why aren't we seeing many wild animals?" Lyle asked as they were sitting by a stream, giving the horses a rest late in the afternoon.

"We're still on the civilization side of the mountain range," she explained. "Besides, most of the deer and elk have moved to the high country. But we should see plenty of them after we cross that switchback straight ahead of us."

Jamie looked around at each of the men, trying to evalute their stamina. She wanted to get to the other side of the first ridge before nightfall. Randy had taken his boots off and was gingerly dipping his feet in the shallow stream they'd just crossed. Fed by freshly melted snow, the water was actually several degrees below freezing, but its swift movement kept it from solidifying into ice. But once the temperatures dropped after sunset, a thin layer of ice would form on top in spite of the water flowing beneath it.

Lyle was lying on a warm, flat rock and pretending to read a book, but Jamie noticed the book kept dropping lower and lower until it rested on his chest, while snores whistled through his partially opened mouth.

Dale seemed to be unaffected by the ride and was studying a nest of bluebirds in a nearby tree.

Lastly, her glance moved to Matt. He stood, leaning against a tree, his back toward her. She couldn't be certain, but she thought he was writing in a small, pocket-size notebook.

He was surprising her. True to his word, she hadn't heard a single complaint from him. He'd kept up and hadn't made any dangerous mistakes although he was obviously not as experienced in the saddle as he had led everyone to believe. He might fool the others, but Jamie and Boots knew a soft seat when they saw one. And that was a criticism only of the way he slid around on the saddle and not the way he filled out his jeans. Jamie's gaze focused on the slightly dirty seat of his tight Levi's. She had no complaints about his anatomy. From the front or from the back, Matt Montana was the best-looking man she'd ever seen. As long as he kept his mouth closed and his hands to himself, she could almost tolerate him.

"If this is National Forest, why isn't it covered with tourists, campers and hikers?" Randy asked as he pulled his socks back on his chilled feet. "We've been riding for hours and haven't seen another person."

Jamie forced her attention back to Randy and explained, "And we probably won't at this time of year. This section of the mountains is totally landlocked. The public may legally use it, but they have no access to it unless they cross private land."

"That sounds like something our government would do," Randy commented.

"You won't hear any complaints from the people around here. Along with all that recreational traffic comes destruction of private property, litter, forest fires and general vandalism of the wilderness."

"But they're more than eager to charge hunters access fees to go into that wilderness and kill the animals." Matt spoke for the first time since they'd stopped for the break.

"If the population of deer and elk isn't reduced each year, we have a huge winter kill. A few seasons ago, we lost ninety percent of our deer and elk herds because there was too little food for too many animals."

"And who's fault is that, I wonder," Matt remarked. "With more and more people building houses, cutting down trees for crops and pastureland, dividing up their ranches into small tracts and selling it to whoever offers them the most money. Can't people see that once all the land is gone, the West is dead?"

"That's easy for you to say!" Jamie declared. "After you get through with your vacation, you'll go back to the city with its millions of houses and apartments. You don't have to live off the land like we do out here. This isn't an *adventure* for us—it's our life. We don't have a lot of jobs or industries...or choices.

Just because our ancestors didn't give up as soon as yours did, but dared to continue farther west doesn't mean you have any right to preach to us about how we use *our* land."

"I didn't mean it that way...exactly."

"Well, that's how it sounded." Jamie tried to calm down. She had no idea why that man had the power to make her so furious. With anyone else, she could carry on a sane conversation. But with Matt, everything turned into an argument.

"None of us *want* to sell," she continued in a more level tone. "But it's expensive to run a ranch nowadays. Many ranchers take the money and start over somewhere else. When things get dangerously tight, it's better to sell than to lose it to the bank. At least we're lucky out here in this part of Colorado because we have people interested in buying. Lots of farmers haven't had that option."

She stood, dusted off the seat of her jeans and headed toward the horses. "Time to hit the trail. We've got a lot of ground to cover before dark."

A chorus of groans followed her, but when she looked around, everyone greeted her with wide, phony grins. Jamie swung into Stormy's saddle easily, then watched while the others mounted. She exchanged a knowing smile with Boots as the other four men pulled themselves stiffly up on their horses' backs, then settled with great care and a lot of grimacing onto their saddles.

The evergreens were tall and thick, stealing the last hour of daylight. They reached the campsite by dusk, but had to pitch the tents by lantern light. To keep the load as light as possible, they'd brought only two tents. It was a simple matter to divide the riders into two groups of three each. Obviously the three friends from New Jersey would take one . . . which meant Jamie, Boots and Matt would share the other.

No problem.

Boots made a campfire, ringed with stones, and set a grill across the flames, while Jamie showed the men how to take care of their horses. After the animals were tethered, groomed and fed a small measure of oats, Jamie and the men returned to the campfire, eager for the heat now that the night chill was setting in.

"What are we having tonight?" she asked Boots.

His face twisted into a crooked grin as he glanced at the four men, none of whom had sat on the big log next to the fire. "Tenderloins," he answered and chuckled.

Matt swaggered closer, his legs suspiciously bowed. "You got that right. So, what's on the menu?"

"Don't joke about such a sensitive matter," Lyle groaned. "I'm hurting in places I didn't even know I had."

Randy added, "I'm hurting in places I wish I didn't have."

"Listen . . . that's a gray wolf howling," Dale said, as usual on a field trip of his own.

"With some help, we could eat a hell of a lot faster," Boots remarked as he stuck a fork into one of the steaks and turned it over, sending a shower of juices sizzling into the fire.

He didn't have to ask twice. Everyone rushed to pitch in to get the meal finished. It was impossible to know if their fever pitch of activity was because they were starving or because they were so anxious to get to bed.

Jamie glanced at the tent she, Boots and Matt would soon be in, and it seemed to shrink before her very eyes. She, for one, wasn't anxious to get to bed.

She handed out the tin plates and flatware, then waved aside the men's polite offer for her to go first. She wasn't in any hurry to finish the meal.

The food disappeared in much less time than it had taken to prepare it. Jamie announced, "Since this is a nonsexist camp, we'll take turns doing the dishes. Lyle and Dale are the lucky ones for night duty and Randy and Matt have breakfast."

"What about you?" Matt asked.

"I'm the trail boss," Jamie said. "I don't wash dishes."

"Afraid of dishpan hands?"

"No, I just don't want to cheat you out of *any* of the real-life experiences of a cowboy on the trail. They didn't have paper plates back then, you know."

"They didn't have down-filled sleeping bags, either, but I'm sure going to appreciate mine tonight," Randy said, stretching his arms over his head. "I've made it through two-a-day workouts during football season and haven't felt this tired."

"Yeah, I could share a sleeping bag with Demi Moore tonight and not be able to do a thing but *sleep*," Lyle groaned. He took the plates and told Dale, "Heat some water and let's get this over with so I can get to bed before my muscles atrophy."

Boots busied himself packing away the food while Lyle and Dale clattered their way through their chore and Randy wandered off into the woods. Jamie remained seated on the log, warming her hands and trying to ignore Matt, who was squatting on the other side of the flames, drinking coffee. She expected, at any moment, for him to begin spouting off about something that would rouse her temper. But as several minutes passed, his silence drew her attention more powerfully than if he'd demanded it.

Across the campfire, Jamie's gaze met Matt's, and a strange warmth flowed through her. In the flickering light, his eyes looked dark and brooding, like one of the romantic heroes in the books she loved. On the trail, he'd lost a little of that cosmopolitan self-confidence she'd found so annoying. She noticed a fresh scratch across his cheek and the exhaustion in his posture, but she also saw a determination not to let anyone know the ride had been more difficult than he'd expected. He was still cocky and outrageous, but with his hair rumpled and his mouth shut, Jamie couldn't keep herself from thinking that he was the most gorgeous man she'd ever seen.

Dale yawned as he wiped his hands with a very damp dishrag. "All finished. I'm going to turn in now. I want to be up in time to see the sunrise and hear the songs of the birds as they wake up."

"We'll all be up to see the sunrise." Jamie's statement drew groans from the other three men. Only Boots, who was always up before dawn, and Dale did not express their dismay.

"If it's all the same to you, I'd rather sleep an extra half hour and miss the sunrise," Randy said, returning to the camp in time to hear the end of the conversation.

"It's up to you, but we're camped within a short hike of a big park and there's usually a large herd of elk there until just after daylight."

"A park?" Lyle asked. "I thought we were deep in the wilderness."

"A park is another name for an open meadow," Jamie explained.

"I'll catch the next one," Randy said, then turned to Dale. "Try not to step on my face when you leave in the morning. That'll be the end of my sleeping bag still snoring."

He began to walk stiffly toward his tent, when Jamie jumped up, anxious for the evening not to end so quickly. All too soon she would be much closer to the man across the flames than she cared to consider, and she wanted to delay bedtime as long as possible.

"Hey, guys," she called. "You're not going to bed so early. It's tradition that we sit around the campfire and tell stories."

The men never hesitated. "Not tonight." Lyle massaged the back of his thighs as he shook his head and said, "This old body is telling me I need rest more than good conversation. Besides, I'm afraid if I sit down, I won't ever get up again."

"If I'm going to be stuck in one position, I'd just as soon it be on my back, tucked into my sleeping bag," Randy added.

Dale nodded. "I think I'd better get some sleep, too. But I do want to go to the park with you in the morning."

Jamie would have tried to change their minds, but a glance at Matt told her he was on to her game and was amused by it. She decided it would only make things worse if she made an issue of it, so she shrugged. "Good night guys. See you in the morning."

They all said their good-nights, then Jamie slowly turned back to the campfire as if she was facing her executioner. He was standing, his arms crossed, obviously enjoying her discomfort. For a long, intense moment, their gazes locked, then he gave her one of his mysterious little half grins and turned toward Boots.

"Need any help with that?" he asked as the older man tied a rope around the top of the duffle bag that contained their food.

"Sure," Boots confirmed concisely. He was never prone to using two words when one would do.

It was a trait Jamie wished more men, especially Matt, would adopt.

Boots handed the bag to Matt and picked up a long, coiled rope. One end had a weight about the size of a golfball tied to it. Shaking that end free, Boots looked up at a branch that was about twenty feet above the ground.

"You'd better step back," Jamie cautioned Matt.

He hoisted the bag over his shoulder and moved a few feet away. "What's he going to do?"

"We have to hang our food and the horses' grain high enough so the wild animals won't get it," she explained. "Especially bears."

"Bears!" Matt scoffed. "You don't really have a problem with bears on these trail rides, do you?"

"I wouldn't call it a problem exactly. We have a pretty healthy population of black bears in this area, but they don't usually bother us. We just don't want to invite them to dinner. That's why we don't keep the food in the tents."

Boots tossed the weighted end over the branch. He motioned for Matt to bring the bag. They worked together to tie the rope securely to the bag, then Boots began backing up and pulling the rope so the sack of food rose out of reach of even the tallest animal. Boots wrapped his end of the rope around the trunk of the tree and tied off.

"I'm going to check on the horses," Jamie said aloud, but as she walked by Boots, she leaned over and whispered, "Whatever you do, make sure your sleeping bag is in the middle."

"Okay," he agreed, but his faded blue eyes teased her that she was overreacting.

It was something she didn't need to have pointed out to her. She already was feeling silly because no other trail ride and no other man had ever made her think twice about sharing a tent. After all, she wasn't going to be sharing her sleeping bag.

Jamie took her time watering the horses, hoping Matt and Boots would be asleep by the time she returned. After she'd double-checked their tethers, she brushed her teeth and washed her face with the water from her canteen.

The camp was quiet and deserted when she came back to it. Even the campfire had been banked. Jamie turned off the lantern Boots had let for her and used her flashlight to find her place inside the tent.

Good to his word, Boots's worn sleeping bag was in the middle with Matt's brand new one to the right and Jamie's to the left. She zipped the door flaps shut, then carefully crawled to her space. Trying to be as quiet as possible, she took the straps off her bag and unrolled it. She removed her coat and folded it to serve as a pillow. Then, after flipping off the flashlight, she unzipped her jeans and eased them down her hips and off her legs before sliding into her sleeping bag.

Boots was already snoring by the time Jamie lay down. It took her another minute to remove her bra without completely taking off her sweatshirt, then she snuggled into the bag's protective warmth.

The music of the night filled the tent as soon as she became still. Outside the tent two owls conversed in their own daunting dialect. A gentle breeze hummed through the needles of the pines, spruces and firs, occasionally causing a cone or a cluster of dead twigs to thump on top of the tent's roof, then slide down the sloping canvas.

Inside the tent, Boots's snoring had settled to a muffled growl. Jamie strained to hear another pattern of breathing. Even with Boots in the middle, she was very aware of the man on the other side of the tent. She could even make out the width of his broad shoulders in the darkness as he lay on his side. He was so close, too close. He made her nervous in a curiously exciting way. On the one hand she dreaded the time they had to spend together; but on the other hand, she wanted him to kiss her again like he had last night in the barn.

He'd been right, she *had* wanted him to kiss her. And once his lips had touched hers, she'd felt her bones . . . and her resistance melt. How could a man's mouth be hard and soft at the same time? His hands were large and felt incredibly good as they caressed her. It hadn't been that she'd objected to him touching her breast, but rather the extremity of her reaction to it. If she had allowed him to continue for another minute, she'd have been tearing off his clothes and tumbling onto the hay in the nearest empty stall.

That realization both excited and alarmed her. She'd read about women who had sexual relationships with men simply for the pleasure of sex. Jamie had never really understood that because the only time she'd made love with a man, she'd been madly in love with him . . . or at least thought she was. He'd told her he would come back after settling his affairs in Atlanta. Little did she know, those "affairs" had included a wife. He'd betrayed her trust and left her doubly cautious of becoming involved with another man. Gradually she'd gotten over him. But she'd vowed never to share a man's bed unless she was sure of his love.

Matt was the first man she'd been attracted to who tempted her to ignore that vow, at least temporarily. If he made love with half the intensity that burned in those dark blue eyes or poured out through his sexy lips, then a night of passion with him would definitely be memorable.

But it would never happen with her. Not because she didn't think she could handle the frivolity of a one-night stand, although it wasn't high on her list of choices, but because he was so sure of himself and his power over her. She refused to be just another conquest whose face and name he wouldn't remember the next morning.

Jamie knew very little about Matt's personal life, but it was clear he didn't have much respect for women. He used them and then left them, just like Duke King.

Jamie told herself it didn't matter. She and Matt would never make a love connection. She was too smart to get involved, especially temporarily, with someone like him. He was an obnoxious, arrogant jerk, remember? He made her crazy every time they tried to have a conversation, remember? He was everything she didn't want in a relationship, remember? He was a guest...remember!

But at the moment all she could think about was that the tent had never been smaller.

Chapter Eight

He should have gone to Club Med. Many of his associates had "fought" writer's block lying on the sand sipping margaritas and letting the Caribbean tickle their toes. Why had he chosen a saddle over a sailboat? It was proof positive he hadn't been thinking clearly.

Matt had planned to take lots of notes of his first impressions and his observations. He'd managed a couple of pages during their break, but he'd been so tired after dinner, he'd fallen asleep almost as soon as he'd zipped up his sleeping bag.

But he hadn't fallen asleep before witnessing the sensual silhouette of Jamie removing her jeans. The sight of her long, slender, naked legs even when they were merely outlined by the dying embers of the campfire through the thin canvas wall, and the thought of her lying so close, had brought on a pain as intense as the dozens of other aches in his abused body.

She'd made her feelings for him perfectly clear. He wasn't a masochist and didn't usually keep setting himself up for rejection. Maybe it was just because she was the only woman for miles around. She was definitely prettier than his horse, but that wasn't exactly strong competition.

He might have accepted that explanation except he didn't want to believe that about himself. If he could get so obsessed by a woman just because she was the only one nearby, it meant he didn't have any standards at all. A man who would hit on anyone simply because they were available wasn't a man of whom he could be proud.

Matt truly didn't believe he was that type of man. Even though he'd never stayed with one woman long enough to let a real relationship develop, it didn't mean he wasn't selective with whom he had an affair. Nowadays, a guy couldn't be too careful. Sometimes he'd slept with a woman just for the sexual release, but he'd always made his intentions perfectly clear and made sure his partner, too, wanted nothing more than carnal pleasure. And sometimes he'd slept with a woman because there was a chance she might become something more than a night's companion.

However, something...some mystical, ethereal *thing*...was always missing. The true test was not whether he wanted to go to sleep next to her while the moon was full and romantic, but whether he wanted to wake up next to her in the morning with the sun glaring in the windows.

With Jamie, neither of those would probably be an option—partly because she and he could never keep from arguing long enough to fall asleep together, and partly because she was always awake before he was.

There was no sun glaring in the windows of the tent when he awoke the next morning. In fact, the curve of the moon was still above the treetops when he sat up and pulled aside the tent flap. The iridescent dial of his watch told him it was only five o'clock. The darn rooster back at the ranch was probably still asleep.

By the light of the freshly stoked campfire Matt could see that both Boots and Jamie were up. And as he watched, Dale left his tent and gingerly sat on the log so he could pull on his boots.

Matt lay back down, but he knew it was only wishful thinking that he might get a few more hours sleep. He hadn't traveled so far or paid so much money to sleep in and miss any part of his "Western adventure." Besides, he didn't want Jamie to know the ride yesterday had almost killed him.

Lord, how could she still walk with that loose, leggy stride he'd noticed the first time they'd met? Didn't those long hours on that hard saddle torture her muscles like it did his? Matt had always prided himself that his body was in peak physical condition. But those years in the gym hadn't prepared him for one day on the back of a horse. Nautilus hadn't invented a machine that exercised the same muscles that Terminator had.

And Matt couldn't imagine a better name for that horse. It was almost as if the animal was playing a game with his rider, lulling him into a false sense of security, then doing something tricky like dodging under a low-lying limb or twisting his head back to take a nip out of Matt's knee.

Matt had tried to make a pact with the horse, a gentleman's agreement, that they wouldn't do anything to damage each other's lives, limbs or reputations before the end of the trail ride. But already

Terminator had reneged, refusing to move forward until Jamie looked back and caught Matt in a situation in which he was clearly not in control. Then Terminator had started forward with an abruptness that almost unseated Matt and proceeded to try to crowd Maybelline off the trail in an attempt to become the leader.

Jamie had stopped and given everyone a lesson on showing the horse who was boss. And while she hadn't actually called Matt's name or even given him a triumphant look, he'd known she was onto his little charade. But he was in too deep. How could he admit to everyone that he wasn't as experienced in the ways of the West as he'd let them believe? He'd lose more than his credibility; he could possibly lose his reputation. And to a man in his line of work, his reputation was more important than a few sore muscles, a scratched cheek and a scabby knee.

With an unenthusiastic moan, he eased his stiff legs into the coldest pair of jeans he'd ever felt. Another form of pioneer birth control, no doubt. The cold temperatures very effectively shrank a man's desires, as well as vital parts of his anatomy.

It was an even greater effort to force his protesting muscles to get him into a standing position and keep him upright.

"God, I'm walking like Hopalong Cassidy," he said to Dale when he joined the other man at the roaring fire.

"At least you can walk," Dale responded. "If it wasn't so cold, I'd take my pants off and rub some liniment on my legs. I feel like I ran the New York Marathon, all uphill, yesterday."

Matt looked enviously at the tube of Ben-Gay lying on the log next to Dale. But to ask to borrow it would mean he'd have to admit he wasn't tough enough. And Matt couldn't bring himself to do that. Damn his pride. But it was too much a part of his character for him to change.

"Oh...good morning," Jamie said to Matt. "I wasn't expecting you to join us."

"Why not?" Matt challenged, his hackles rising at her condescending attitude. "I got as much sleep as you did."

She shrugged as if it didn't matter to her one way or the other and poured some coffee into a thermos. "We're leaving in about five minutes. It's not but about a half mile from here."

A half mile! Matt didn't say it aloud, but inside, his feet were sending a panicky message to his brain. *A half mile in these boots? We'd rather you just cut us off now and get it over with.* Matt glanced down at the exotic boots he'd chosen with such care. But he'd picked them because they looked so cowboy cool rather than because they felt good. And now he was living to regret it.

"We'll be back about eight," Jamie told Boots after she finished off her biscuit with a very unfeminine speed. She packed the thermos, more biscuits and a couple of pairs of binoculars into a drawstring bag which she hung over her shoulder. "Ready?" she asked Matt and Dale. "Don't forget your flashlights."

They had no choice but to take their flashlights from their pockets, nod with forced eagerness, follow her into the darkness of the forest and hope she had either a good sense of direction or a good memory so they would someday return to camp. Matt's spirit was willing, but his feet were weak, so he fell back into third position as they walked on and on.

In spite of the rough terrain, Jamie made almost no sound as she moved confidently forward. To Matt's ears, he and Dale sounded like a herd of bull elephants stampeding through the jungle. To his great annoyance, no matter how carefully he placed his feet, the rustle of dried leaves, the snapping of twigs or the clatter of rocks haunted his steps. And when Jamie glanced back with a whispered "shh", it only made him clumsier.

Finally, when Matt was about ready to collapse to the ground and tell them to leave him and pick him up on the way back or just to let him die with his boots off, Jamie slowed down.

"It's through those trees," she informed the men in a barely audible voice. "We're downwind, so they can't smell us. But we have to be *very* quiet or we'll spook them." She turned off her flashlight. "We'll have to go the rest of the way without these."

Matt thought she was asking a lot. If he couldn't walk quietly with his path illuminated by a flashlight, how could she possibly expect him to sneak up on a herd of elk when he couldn't see a foot in front of him?

But when he turned off his light, he was surprised to see that dawn was already beginning its mutiny of the night sky. Although only a couple of shades lighter than before, he could make out the shapes of the trees and the people in front of him.

They crossed the last few dozen yards with amazing silence. "Try to stay beside a tree," Jamie whispered. "Their eyesight isn't very good. They can see movement much better than they can recognize shapes, so try to blend with the forest and freeze if one looks in your direction."

Matt still didn't see any animals, or even a meadow for that matter, but he followed Jamie's lead, moving from tree to tree, then crouching as they walked up a small incline. When she got down on her hands and knees, then stretched out on her stomach, Matt and Dale exchanged a pained glance, then forced their uncooperative muscles to do the same.

The hike had left him breathless, so it took a few minutes for his heart to stop pounding in his ears and his lungs to catch up with the thin air. Once he could hear over his body's hysterical complaining, he could hear the silence of the morning. His intellect told him a person can't actually *hear* silence, but his artistic soul believed it was possible.

There could be no such thing as true silence except in a vacuum. Just as the color white was the presence of all colors, real silence was magnified by the presence of many sounds. Scattered, sporadic chirps could be heard as the birds began stirring on their roosts. The scratch of squirrels scampering along tree limbs and their staccato barking when something intruded on their area echoed in the stillness. A porcupine rustled through the underbrush, wandering along the edge of the forest only a few feet in front of the prone people. They didn't move, and the small awkward-looking animal never even glanced in their direction.

As the sky continued to lighten, Matt saw there was a fog or some sort of heavy mist hanging low in the meadow. He continued to peer into its whiteness, trying to see what had been so important that he'd had to get up at a time that should be officially banned from alarm clocks.

He heard them before he saw them, large, powerful hooves pawing the earth, strong teeth tearing the grass from its roots and grinding it into cud, the singsong call of the cow elk talking to their calves and their higher pitched answer.

Slowly, the mist began to lift, revealing the abstract image of legs. No bodies, just legs, hundreds of them.

Out of the corner of his eye, he saw Jamie had her camera trained on the odd sight. She clicked the shutter, advanced the film and waited for the next shot.

As the mists began to clear, Matt could make out the shape of the animals' heads as they grazed on the tall grass. Gradually their dark bellies came into view, then the rest of their huge bodies. Matt had seen elk in zoos, but their size and magnificence hadn't made such an impression behind the wire mesh fences.

For a few minutes between the time it was light enough to see them and when the sun actually began peeking through the trees, the park was filled with animals. The calves romped with each other while their mothers continued feeding. Slightly separated from the main herd, twenty or thirty bull elk of various sizes and ages concentrated on the necessity of eating. Matt knew from his research that elk and deer had to forage almost continuously in order to get enough to eat.

Matt also knew that in the fall, the males wouldn't be banding together so peacefully. Regardless of size or age, it would be every bull for himself during the brief, but intense mating period. Brother would fight brother, and father would fight son for the right to ''own'' the most cows.

Matt couldn't resist glancing at Jamie. It was nature's perfect plan that the males should dominate the females. Far be it from him to go against something that had been working for millions of years.

Jamie must have intercepted his thoughts because she turned her head and looked directly into his eyes.

Maybe it was the dark or the fog or the excitement or even the exhaustion, but Matt hadn't realized how close they were lying to each other. Suddenly the sounds of the elk and the birds faded into the background as a different kind of silence enveloped them. He could see the thick fringe of surprisingly dark lashes around her clear blue eyes. Her cheeks were flushed from the chill still lingering in the mountain air and her blond hair feathered across her forehead in wind-ruffled bangs. She was wearing no makeup and you could hardly call her puffy down jacket high fashion. But never, in his whole life, had he seen a woman look so beautiful in the morning.

And never had he wanted to kiss a pair of lips more than he wanted to kiss hers. Under any other circumstances, if she were any other person, he would have given in to temptation without a second thought. However, his body was already in enough pain. He didn't need another fist in the stomach or more pent-up sexual tension that had no hope of being released.

Her gaze lowered to his mouth, moving over his lips with such thoroughness he could almost feel it. Was it his imagination or had she leaned closer? Her eyes were as soft and misty as the meadow when she lifted her gaze. If ever he'd seen someone wanting to be kissed, it was Jamie Kimball. And he desperately wanted to comply.

But he'd been wrong before.

Matt caught sight of Dale a few feet on the other side of Jamie and was reminded they weren't alone. Maybe she felt safe flirting with him with someone else so near. Matt wouldn't have thought Jamie was a tease, but then, the more he got to know her, the less he knew her. Even in his own mind that was confusing, but that was exactly the emotion he felt when he was around her. It was an emotion he wasn't accustomed to feeling.

Abruptly he looked back at the park, intentionally breaking the spell.

"They're gone!" he exclaimed aloud, surprised to discover that the elk had melted into the underbrush. He was amazed that that many large creatures could move so silently, so quickly. It was as if they hadn't existed at all except in his imagination.

Jamie rolled over and sat up. "Once the sun comes up, they move into the dark timber. It's cooler there...and safer." She took out the thermos and poured them each a cup of coffee, then handed them the individually wrapped biscuits.

"Would you send me a copy of the photographs you took?" Dale asked. "I'd be glad to pay for them."

"Sure I will. And don't worry about the cost. I can get double prints free."

Matt halfway listened to the conversation as she and Dale continued talking about the wildlife and the ecosystem of the forest. Mostly he watched her, waiting for some sign that their earlier silent connection had actually happened.

But Jamie barely glanced his way, almost pointedly cutting him out of the dialogue. Matt dragged his gloved fingers through his hair and shook his head. There was no doubt about it. He was losing his mind . . . and it was all her fault.

She stood and repacked the thermos and their trash. "Let's head back to camp. We need to be on the trail by nine."

Dale was distracted by a cluster of wildflowers, so Matt stepped out behind Jamie as she began the return hike. He was concentrating on how tight his boots had become and how his aching thighs were making his legs feel like cooked spaghetti, and not on the details of the trail. When a doe leapt out of the underbrush almost directly under Jamie's feet, she jumped back. Matt didn't react as quickly. Before he had time to stop, she was plastered against his body. His arms automatically wrapped around her to steady them both. His face was buried in the soft mass of her hair, filling his nostrils with her sweet, special fragrance. How could she smell so good after a hard day in the saddle and a night in a sleeping bag, especially when he felt grubby after one morning without a shower and shave?

For a full minute she didn't move away. He felt her tremble beneath his protective embrace, and she seemed to relax against him. Then as suddenly as she moved backward, she pulled away and stepped forward.

"Uh...sorry," she said, her voice low and suspiciously shaky. "I can't believe she let us walk right up on her like that."

Dale caught up with them in time to hear Jamie's last statement. Without actually touching any of the bushes, he began peering over and under the clustered branches. "I'll bet she left a fawn behind and is trying to play decoy so we'll follow her."

"Yes, probably," Jamie agreed, forcing her eyes to look away from Matt. She went through the motions of leaning forward to look under the bushes, but it was obvious her mind wasn't focused on finding the baby deer.

"Look! There they are," Dale exclaimed. "It's twins."

Matt moved behind Jamie and gazed over her shoulder at the two incredibly tiny spotted fawns trying very hard to be invisible on their bed of dried leaves. And they would have been practically impossible to notice beneath the dappling of the sun through the leaves had the people not known almost exactly where to look.

The little animals returned the humans' stares with equal curiosity. There was no fear in the large, round, brown velvet eyes that gazed back. They were too young to know the difference between two-legged and four-legged animals.

"Don't touch *anything*," Jamie cautioned in a soothing whisper. "Let's slip away so their mother will come back."

"Would you take a picture of them for my class?" Dale asked.

Jamie complied, then moved away, being careful not to brush up against Matt even though he was very close behind her. She did, however, glance sideways at him through her lowered lashes, and there was more fear in her eyes than there had been in the fawns'.

Was she afraid of him? Matt couldn't imagine why she would be. She'd certainly never shown any hesitation to stand up to him.

Matt frowned. He didn't like the idea that she might, in any way, fear him. Her audacity and spirit were two of the things that fascinated him the most. He knew dozens, possibly hundreds of beautiful women. But he'd never met anyone with such fierce courage, and he didn't want to believe there was anything that intimidated her.

By the time they reached the camp, all hints of a possible chink in her confident armor had disappeared. As soon as everyone ate breakfast and washed the dishes, she supervised the dismantlement of the camp, including the removal of all signs of human occupation. Just as she'd stated, they were in the saddle by nine o'clock.

"The trail's a little trickier today," she told them. "So be careful and pay extra attention."

If Matt thought he hurt while walking, he hadn't known the meaning of pain. He almost had to bite his lip to keep from moaning with every step Terminator took. The muscles of his thighs and calves were screaming in protest at being stretched around the horse's broad body. Even worse, there were certain tender parts of his male anatomy that were so badly bruised, he was beginning to wonder if it might forever affect his chances for fatherhood.

Not that he had any plans to become a father. So far, he hadn't seen any good arguments for bringing more children into the world. But, dammit, he didn't want that option to be taken away from him by a horse who seemed determined to remove Matt from the saddle.

When Matt could get his mind off his own aches and lift his gaze from the ever-fascinating sight of Jamie's lithe body rolling with her horse's gait in front of him, he could appreciate the spectacular mountain peaks that were growing closer by the mile. Even with the sun beating down on them, the air was definitely chillier, and everyone except Jamie and Boots, who wore down-filled vests, kept their jackets on.

More wild animals were sighted that day, and Dale gave everyone a running commentary on the types of trees and birds they were seeing. When they stopped for lunch, Boots showed the men how to catch rainbow trout out of the stream, using branches for poles and hand-tied flies for bait. By the time they left the area, Boots had packed ten fat, colorful trout in an insulated, waterproof bag where he kept the perishables, and everyone was looking forward to having them for dinner. Matt was pleased to have contributed three, especially since they were the first three fish he'd ever caught. In fact, it was the first time he'd ever gone fishing.

All morning, clouds had been moving in from the north, first as friendly-looking puffs, then as larger, bottom-heavy thunderheads. When a few fat raindrops fell, Jamie turned up her collar and pulled her buff-colored cowboy hat lower to shield her face, but she didn't slow the pace.

The other men untied the yellow slickers from behind their saddles and pulled them on, but Matt decided he could be as tough as Jamie was. He zipped his jacket up and tipped his head forward so the rain drained off the front of his hat's brim instead of drizzling down his neck. He tried to ignore the watermarks on the leather of his jacket that would probably leave permanent spots. He tried to ignore the chill that was soaking through his wet jeans and all the way to his bones. He tried to ignore the slickness of the saddle seat that made him feel even more insecure on Terminator's back. He tried to ignore the sneaking suspicion that Jamie didn't have a clue where she was going, but was determined that they all die of pneumonia.

It wasn't until the rain became a steady downpour that she finally stopped and dismounted. She led her horse under a huge natural rock amphitheater-shaped formation that offered protection from the storm on three sides and over the top. As everyone crowded together, shivering and seeking each other's warmth, Matt had to admit that Jamie had done a good job of getting them to what was probably one of the few places on this mountainside where men, horses and equipment could find shelter while waiting out the storm.

He also tried to ignore the way her cotton shirt had become transparent in the rain. The soaked material clung to her like a second skin, and even her lacy, surprisingly feminine bra did little to provide modesty.

The rosy tips of her nipples were clearly detailed to everyone who noticed.

Matt glanced around and saw he wasn't the only man to be paying close attention to Jamie's chest as she lifted her arms to remove her hat and wring the excess water out of her long hair. Only Boots was too busy with his mule's pack to be ogling the unexpected display of mother nature at her best.

Jamie was oblivious to the stares as she tilted her head while she plaited her hair into a thick braid. Her gaze was focused on the sheet of rain that was pouring off the flat protrusion of rock that was serving as their roof.

Matt noticed Randy nudging Lyle and whispering something that Matt couldn't hear, but could certainly guess it would never have been said had Buck been their trail master. Even Dale was peering over the top rim of his fogged-up glasses with a sort of fascinated curiosity as if he were studying an interesting specimen of a near-extinct creature.

Rage boiled inside Matt. How dare they leer at Jamie like that! She didn't deserve such disrespect. His hands clenched into fists. They longed to punch those horny teachers in their collective intellectual noses.

Instead, he unzipped his jacket and took it off. Stepping in front of her, carefully blocking the others' line of vision, he placed the jacket around her shoulders.

She looked up at him in surprise. "Thanks, but I'm not cold."

He let his gaze flick over her breasts with eloquent persuasion. He even resisted the urge to take a good, long look of her ample charms himself. Feeling uncharacteristically chivalrous, he just wanted her to cover herself.

Jamie glanced down and gasped. She crossed her arms over her chest as an embarrassed flush crept up her neck and stained her cheeks.

Another even more obscure emotion stirred within him. He didn't want her to be unhappy. If he could cushion her from even a moment's discomfort, he would feel he'd accomplished something important. As he looked down at her beautiful, blushing face, a protective instinct he'd never known he possessed overwhelmed him.

Not that she would ever allow anyone to be her protector. But that, in itself, made her all the more appealing and made him all the more determined to take care of her. At least until this trail ride was over.

Matt pulled the lapels closed over her arms. The jacket was much too large for her so it effectively covered everything that needed to be covered.

"Thanks," she repeated, but this time the word was soft and whispery...and incredibly sexy. She lifted her face toward his, and the expression in her eyes held the same confused longing it had earlier that morning.

She'd fooled him before. But this time he was positive. If he wanted to savor those moist, full lips, he knew she would not only let him...she would kiss him back. But would it be because she wanted the kiss or because she appreciated his jacket?

It surprised him that her motivations mattered. Matt didn't want her because she was grateful or confused. He wanted her only if she wanted him. Jamie was not like the other women he'd dated. He didn't know her nearly as well as he'd like to, but he did

know that she wouldn't give herself to someone lightly.
The man would have to mean something special to her.

And, Matt realized with a strange tightening in his
chest that was even more powerful than the desire in
his groin, he wanted Jamie to think *he* was special.

Chapter Nine

Jamie retrieved her own jacket from her saddlebags, but she had to force herself to put it on. Actually, it was because she didn't want to take Matt's jacket off.

She'd been genuinely touched by what he'd done. It was a gesture of generosity she would never have expected of him. It would have been more in keeping with his personality to have taken advantage of the impromptu peep show to get his macho kicks. It wouldn't have surprised her at all if he'd led the pack of wolves leering at her near nakedness. Instead, he had pointedly avoided staring at her and even shielded her from the others.

Her cheeks burned again at the thought that all the men had probably gotten an eyeful. When she'd looked down and seen her nipples fairly glowing through the wet white material, she'd wanted to melt into the ground. But Matt's body had been a solid wall between her and the others, giving her back her modesty.

That wasn't the Matt Montana she knew and disliked. Duke King would never have been so kind.

With a last deep breath, filled with the distinctly masculine fragrance of leather . . . and Matt, she replaced his jacket with her own, carefully keeping her back to the men until she was zipped up to a modest level.

She handed Matt his jacket, not quite able to meet his eyes. She really hated it when he did something nice. Of all the things in the world that she didn't want, liking Matt was at the top of her list.

The men played poker, and Jamie kept her distance, standing next to the overhang and watching the rain sluice off the edge like a waterfall.

It was mid-afternoon by the time the rain stopped. The clouds lingered, however, threatening to dump another deluge on them.

Regaining control of her scattered wits, she said, "I need some fresh air. I don't know what smells worse, wet men or wet horses."

She checked Stormy's cinch and wiped the saddle seat with a bandanna she found in her coat pocket. Leading him out from under the rock ledge, Jamie stepped into the stirrup and mounted.

"Let the horses have a loose rein so they can pick their footing," she informed the men. "We'll take it a little slower, but we should still make it to the lake by dark."

The rocks were slippery under Stormy's hooves, but she was experienced with finding the best path. The other horses trusted Stormy just as the men were trusting Jamie.

They'd been back on the trail for less than an hour with only one peak left between them and their destination, when the path narrowed until it was little more than a ledge of rock. But Stormy and the other horses and mules had traveled it a half dozen times, so they didn't hesitate.

Jamie glanced back at the men and saw they were more nervous than the animals. "Trust your horses," she called over her shoulder. "Just sit tight and let them do the work. It's not as dangerous as it seems."

The men nodded even though their expressions showed they weren't totally convinced. But almost as soon as Jamie had turned forward again, she heard a rumble that made the hair stand up on the back of her neck.

Small pebbles trickled down the rocky slope, heralding a much more frightening event.

"Rock slide!" Boots shouted just as Jamie urged Stormy forward at a faster pace.

The mare, too, had recognized the danger and was moving more quickly of her own accord with Maybelline crowding close behind. Jamie knew there was a clearing just around the corner. If only they could reach it before any large rocks fell on the riders.

But a thick layer of mud and runoff water from the earlier downpour provided a slick, fast conveyance for the boulders that were tumbling down the mountain. As Jamie rounded the curve, she heard the roar increase, along with the clatter of stone against stone. She couldn't see the men, but she could hear their shouts and the panicky screams of the horses. As soon as she reached the clearing, she whirled Stormy and Maybelline around, waiting anxiously for the men to burst around the corner.

Her heart stopped as she watched. When Terminator with Matt clinging to the saddlehorn came into sight, she heaved a big sigh, but her relief was short-lived.

"It came down right behind me," he gasped when he was able to pull Terminator to a stop next to her. He leaned down and patted the horse's sweat-frothed neck. "If it wasn't for this horse's quick reflexes, we'd have been smashed by a boulder the size of Hulk Hogan."

"What about the others?"

"I couldn't see. The rocks were crashing down all around us and Terminator blasted off."

They waited a few more seconds, but as the time stretched, Jamie's heart sank. Something was wrong.

"I've got to go back." She dismounted and tied Stormy and Maybelline to a couple of sturdy trees.

"I'll go with you," Matt stated, and after securing Terminator, he caught up with her as she reached the trail.

Jamie was glad to have him with her because she didn't know what to expect as she retraced her steps on the path. The rumbling had stopped, but she could hear shouts from what sounded like several locations.

Rounding the corner, she slid to a stop, her way blocked by a wall of rock. It looked too unstable for her to try to climb, so she called to whoever might hear her, "Are you okay over there?"

"Jamie! Thank God you're alive," Lyle shouted.

"Matt's over here with me. We're fine," Jamie said. "How are the other guys?"

"Not good," Lyle answered. "A big rock took Dale over the edge. Boots and Randy are trying to get down to him while I stay here with the horses."

"Oh, no," Jamie cried. She peered over the edge and could barely see some movement several hundred feet below. She immediately began picking her way down the mountain. When Matt started to follow, she told him to go back to the horses and bring a couple of ropes and the first-aid kit that were packed on Maybelline.

Randy was kneeling next to Dale while Boots was trying to calm Dale's horse who was trying to struggle to his feet. Jamie was out of breath from her quick descent as she dropped to her knees. Dale's eyes were closed and his face was deathly pale.

"Is he . . . ?" she asked.

Randy shook his head. "No, but he's in a lot of pain."

Jamie touched Dale's neck and was relieved to find his pulse was strong. His eyelids fluttered, then opened and he looked up at her.

"What happened?" he asked.

"You were caught in a mud slide," she explained. "How are you feeling?"

"I've felt better."

He started to move, but Jamie's hands on his shoulders forced him to lie still.

"Don't move. We need to check you for injuries." She began running her hands down his arms. "Where does it hurt?"

He shifted his legs and winced. "My left leg is broken, I think."

Jamie checked his rib cage, then moved down to his legs. When she touched his ankle, she could feel the bone angled crookedly. "Yes, I think you're right."

She pulled a knife out of her pocket and, as gently as possible, cut his pants leg open.

"Are you going to set it?" Randy asked.

"This isn't a John Wayne movie," she answered as she studied the edge of the bone that was pushing against his skin. "It isn't just a matter of pulling the bone back in place and setting it. Help me get his boots off."

Matt arrived, carrying one rope, the first-aid kit and a blanket. The other rope he'd tied to a rock beside the trail before dropping it over the edge.

Jamie took the blanket from him and covered Dale. "I'm going to call for a helicopter. You just lie here. I'll be back in a few minutes." To Randy she said, "Would you take care of his cuts? And be sure he doesn't try to move."

"You're going to *call?*" Matt asked. "I didn't notice any pay phones along the way."

"I carry a shortwave radio in my saddlebags for emergencies," Jamie explained.

"Why don't you order a few pepperoni pizzas while you're at it," Dale managed to joke through gritted teeth.

Randy looked at the first-aid kit and paled. "But some of his cuts might need stitches. I can handle sprains and muscle pulls, but I'm not too good with wounds that bleed."

"Then move out of the way." Matt squatted down next to Dale and opened the kit. "Growing up in an inner city acquainted me with the sight of blood," he said as he took out a package of butterfly bandages and began applying them to Dale's worst cuts.

Jamie felt confident she was leaving Dale in good hands. Who would have suspected that Matt would be the strong one, she thought. With a last glance at Dale, she walked over to Boots where he was still talking soothingly to Dale's horse. She could see by the way the mare's foreleg dangled that her leg was broken and she was bleeding profusely from several severe cuts. "It looks bad."

"It is."

"Do you want to take care of her or should I?" she asked Boots.

"I'll do it."

Jamie's eyes filled with tears as she stroked the bay mare's muddy neck. The horse was trembling with pain and fear, but she recognized the gentle touch and rubbed her black velvety nose against Jamie's cheek. "I'm sorry, Lady," Jamie murmured, her heart aching for the beautiful mare. Although she was a few years past her prime, she'd always been a sweet-tempered, reliable mount for even the rankest beginners and had produced some outstanding foals, including her own mare, Stormy.

When Jamie saw Boots draw his revolver from the holster he always wore on the trail rides, she fled. She could have done it if necessary, but killing animals, even when they were in pain was one of the most difficult parts of being a rancher. She climbed back up, pulling herself along with the rope. She had barely reached the top when the crack of the gun echoed through the canyon.

Jamie's shoulders slumped, and she had to struggle to swallow past the lump in her throat. But a man's life was more important than grieving over a horse, so she hurried as fast as she dared along the narrow trail, then broke into a jog across the clearing to where the horses were tethered.

It took her a couple of minutes to hook the radio to the battery and set it up, then a few more minutes to get someone at the ranch to answer her distress call. After giving her father their coordinates and detailing the specifics of the clearing where the helicopter would have to land, she made another trip down the mountain.

Matt was sitting on a rock next to Dale, keeping up a conversation even though Dale kept trying to doze off. But every time his eyelids started to droop, Matt switched subjects and practically forced Dale to join the discussion.

When he looked up at Jamie, she gave him an appreciative smile. He answered with an offhanded shrug that attempted to dismiss his contributions to the emergency. But Jamie knew the importance of Matt's calm, efficient handling of the situation, and she was very glad he'd been there with her.

They could hear the powerful blades slicing through the air as the helicopter approached. Jamie had returned to the clearing to flag them down if necessary, because the clouds were still hanging low over the mountains, and she was afraid they'd have trouble finding the landing site. But the rescue chopper's pilot found the large open space and settled onto it. Jamie stood at the horses' heads, trying to calm them as they danced and fidgeted at the terrifying noise.

When the paramedics leapt out of the helicopter, carrying their bags and a lightweight basket they would use to lift the patient out of the canyon, Jamie led them down to where Matt was still trying desperately to entertain Dale and keep him conscious.

After a quick check of his vital signs, followed by a more thorough inspection of his injuries, the paramedics decided it would be safe to move him. They strapped him into the basket, then brought the helicopter over the spot where Dale was to be lifted out. The chopper hovered overhead, whipping the trees and sending the dried leaves into dancing whirlwinds as the medics on the ground attached the cables to the basket, then gave the all-clear sign.

Slowly, Dale floated out of the canyon and over the treetops while everyone on the ground rushed to get back up so they could assist with the landing in the clearing. Once the helicopter was back on earth with Dale safely off to one side, the hospital crew loaded him onto a regular gurney and hooked him up to some monitoring machines.

Jamie watched helplessly, trying not to get in the way, but also being available when they needed an extra hand. As they were loading Dale into the helicopter, she hung back until he called to her.

The medics moved aside to let her talk to him. She took his hand as she said, "Dale, I'm really sorry this happened. If I can do anything, anything at all..."

He smiled. "It wasn't your fault. You warned us about the dangers of the trail. I enjoyed it right up until that rock took me and Lady over the edge." His expression grew sober. "And I'm really sorry about her. She was a fine horse."

Jamie nodded, but couldn't speak through her tears...tears of gratitude that Dale was going to be okay, tears of sorrow for the loss of a good horse and tears of exhaustion.

"But I'll be back as soon as I'm better," Dale continued. He opened his other hand and there was a large stone that strongly resembled a tooth. "Matt found this and gave it to me. Isn't it terrific?"

She must not have looked properly impressed, because he added, "It's a dinosaur tooth, probably a tyrannosaurus rex. See the tearing edge? It was definitely a meat eater, and I'm coming back to look for the rest of him next summer."

Jamie looked down at the tooth, then at Dale's beaming face. Finally, her gaze lifted to Matt and she sent him a silent thanks.

There wasn't room for Randy and Lyle to go with Dale in the helicopter, so the remaining trail riders stood in the clearing and waved as the chopper rose well above the trees, then disappeared into the clouds.

The silence after it was gone and the emotional plummet left everyone standing numbly for several minutes. It was Lyle who spoke first.

"Will we start back right away or wait until morning?" he asked.

Jamie looked at her watch. Normally, there would be about three hours of sunshine left, but the cloud cover would cut that time in half. "I think you guys should get started as soon as possible. You should be able to make it back to the stream where we had lunch if you push, or at least to where we waited out the rain. It's mostly downhill, so you should make it down by noon tomorrow."

"*We* guys?" Randy asked. "Aren't you coming back with us?"

Jamie glanced at Randy and Lyle who were obviously anxious to get out of the mountains to be with their friend, then at Matt who was trying very hard not to let his disappointment show. "No, we can't," she answered. "The rock slide cut us off."

"But you're going to catch up with us tomorrow, right?" Lyle persisted.

Jamie lifted her gaze to meet Matt's. "We're going on."

"We don't have to," he said, offering her a way out of her commitment to him.

"You paid for a five-day trail ride, and there's no reason you shouldn't get it. There's no reason we can't finish." She paused and tilted her chin up a few degrees in an unconsciously defensive gesture. "That is unless you don't trust me to get us through."

The corners of his lips twitched, then, slowly, a grin stretched across his handsome face. "Sure, if you're willing, I'd like to keep going."

"Boots, you can take Randy and Lyle back down, and then pick up Matt and me on Friday at our regular meeting place on the other side of the mountain. I'll call and let you know what time. Okay?"

"Sure."

"We'll need to split our supplies." She had to force herself not to glance at Matt as she said, "I suppose we can get by with one tent." She sincerely hoped he wasn't reading more into that than simple practicality.

They completely unloaded Maybelline, and Boots took what supplies he needed. Then they had to climb down the mountain and back up again to get around the avalanche, carrying the supplies taken from Maybelline's pack. They unpacked Boots's mule, divided the food and cooking utensils and helped him repack his supplies.

"We need fewer supplies, so I'll be able to take the extra saddle back," Boots said.

"Good, and break the news about Lady gently to Dad. She was one of his favorites."

"Yeah, I know."

"You and the guys should get on your way," Jamie told Boots. "Matt and I will be able to handle getting our stuff back to our horses. We'll just make camp there, then take our time getting to the lake tomorrow."

"You'll be fine."

Boots's confidence in her was very comforting, and she gave him a little hug. "So will you." To Randy and Lyle she said, "I hope you two will give the Rocky K another chance."

"Sure, we'll be back with Dale," Randy told her, and Lyle nodded his agreement.

They finished their goodbyes and Matt and Jamie circled the rockslide for the last time. They were both very tired by the time they reached the clearing. With a minimum of dialogue, they managed to get the tent raised and to fry the fish he'd caught earlier. As they lingered around the campfire, soaking in its warmth, Jamie could barely keep her eyes open, and she noticed Matt was doing more than his share of yawning.

But as soon as they began rolling out their sleeping bags in the tent, Jamie became wide awake...and very aware of the man with whom she would be sharing that tent.

"Uh...I'd better check on the horses one last time," she muttered and fled the small confines.

A stream ran along the edge of the clearing, and the horses and mule were able to reach it from the length of their tether ropes. They'd been fed and groomed, and there wasn't really any reason for her to stay with them. However, thirty minutes later she was still sitting on a large flat rock, leaning against the trunk of a lodgepole pine and watching the animals nibble on the knee-high grass. When even they stopped eating and began to doze, Jamie knew she could avoid bedtime no longer. Besides, the cold was starting to cut through her jeans.

She was shivering as she crawled into the tent, but she tried to be quiet. It was too dark to see if he was asleep, but Matt didn't move when she zipped the flap shut, then quickly moved to her side of the small area. She glanced at him again, then unzipped her pants and started to pull them down.

"Need any help?"

She jerked the jeans back over her hips. "I thought you were asleep."

"I was. Until a herd of elephants came stomping in."

"Sorry. I tried to be quiet."

He shifted in his sleeping bag, and Jamie wasn't sure if he was trying to go back to sleep or not. She knew there was no way he could actually see her nakedness in the thick darkness, but she slid into her sleeping bag before removing her jeans and bra. So far she'd made do with spot washing, but tomorrow she was determined to take an actual bath, even if it would be a very quick plunge into the frigid lake.

"I thought the tent would seem larger without Boots," Matt commented, obviously still awake.

"So did I." Jamie zipped the bag's side all the way up, then lay on her back, trying to pretend the man lying a couple of feet away from her was no one special. But it was becoming increasingly difficult to remember all the reasons why he annoyed her. "Dale was thrilled about that tooth fossil. That was a nice thing for you to do."

There was a slight pause before Matt answered, "I just happened to see it when I was standing there. I figured it would mean more to him than it would to me."

"Well, I wanted to thank you for saving the day. The Rocky K can't afford unhappy customers. It's bad enough to have an accident on one of our rides, but when someone gets hurt, it can ruin a business like ours."

"It could have been worse," he said, his voice projecting upward so Jamie knew he was lying on his back, staring up but seeing nothing just as she was.

Actually, there was something anonymous about talking in total darkness, almost as if the conversation wasn't really taking place and that everything that was said would be forgotten with the light of day. Just like a slumber party, night inspired the sharing of secrets and the bonding of the participants.

"I wish I'd thought about the possibility of an avalanche," she mused aloud. "We could have spent the night at the rock wall and taken that trail tomorrow morning. Maybe it would have been a little drier."

"The accident wasn't your fault," Matt stated with a firm absoluteness. "No one, not even your father, could have predicted what happened today."

Jamie wished she could believe that. But, of course, hindsight was always clearer than foresight.

"I may have been a skeptic when we started this ride," Matt continued, "but you've convinced me you can handle anything. I thought you did an excellent job of coordinating Dale's rescue and keeping everyone calm."

Jamie turned her head and looked toward him even though she could barely make out the rugged outline of his profile. "You helped a lot. I thought Randy was going to lose his lunch when he looked at the blood."

"I haven't spent much time around cows and horses, but I've seen more than my share of fights."

"Out in the streets of Chicago?"

He didn't answer for so long, that Jamie thought he hadn't heard her question.

"No," he said, his voice low and harsh, "in my living room. My parents didn't get along too well. That was when Barbara still lived with us."

"Barbara?"

"My mother."

From his tone Jamie sensed there was a lot of pain and anger in those memories. There were at least a dozen questions Jamie wanted to ask, but it was such a sensitive subject, she knew he'd have to be the one to volunteer any information.

Apparently, he'd said as much as he wanted to about it, because he rolled to his side, facing away from her and said, "We don't have to get up at the crack of dawn tomorrow, do we?"

"No, we can sleep in . . . at least until six."

"Is that a.m. or p.m.?"

"Take your choice," Jamie answered, not making any effort to stifle a huge yawn as total exhaustion began to overtake her. "It's your vacation."

Her yawn was contagious and he answered with one of his own. "Some vacation," he muttered, but there was no regret in his tone. "I've never worked so hard in my life."

Chapter Ten

She filled his senses with her beauty and sweetness. Hair, soft as rabbit fur, tickled his cheek. Lips, swollen from a night of passion, pressed against his neck, her warm breath caressing his skin as she slept.

She shifted, burrowing closer against him and sighed with the pleasurable memories of their lovemaking.

Duke's arms tightened. Soon his work would be finished in this town, and he would have to leave. A pang of regret tightened in his chest. He'd known many women, not all in the Biblical sense, but certainly he'd had his choice. He loved women, not individually, but as a group, and he'd never been tempted to settle down with just one.

Until now.

He rubbed his face against her silky spun-gold hair. He had no doubt he would tire of her eventually. No woman held his interest long. He didn't trust females any more than he trusted a coiled rattlesnake.

But this particular woman had somehow slipped through his defenses. He wouldn't mind spending a few more nights with her. Hell, he wouldn't even mind spending a few more days with her, and that was something he'd never felt about a woman before.

It wasn't like he was tempted to stay with her forever. There was no chance of that. Their life-styles were too different. She was rooted in this small town, and he had never known a real home. Nor did he want one. He was perfectly satisfied with things the way they were. And that didn't include a permanent female.

Duke King had no room in his life for a woman. Other men might make fools of themselves, but he would never fall in love. No woman would ever hurt him. And he made sure that would never happen by always leaving, before his heart got involved. He'd been shot a half-dozen times, dragged by a horse, stabbed and left for dead. His body had taken every sort of punishment and abuse imaginable... but his heart had never been touched.

The woman moved again, and Duke kissed the top of her head. Yes, it was time to move on. This lady was more dangerous than any villain he'd ever faced. Her weapons were sheathed in velvety soft skin and warm, gentle eyes.

Duke looked down at her peacefully sleeping form. Memories of their lovemaking aroused him, and he knew he couldn't leave without one more kiss. Just one more. Then he'd be on his way out of town and out of her life... forever.

He lifted her chin and let his mouth gently touch her lips. They responded instantly, warming to his kiss and responding with a passion that swept thoughts of leaving out of his mind. All he wanted was to kiss her and...

The lips beneath his were real. The realization brought Matt awake with a start. He pulled back and looked down at Jamie. She was sound asleep.

Sometime during the night, they had rolled together, meeting on the neutral ground in the middle of the tent. She was snuggled up against him as if she was used to sleeping next to a man.

The thought aroused an emotion in him that was suspiciously similar to jealousy. But he knew it couldn't possibly be that. Matt Montana was never possessive. Nothing or no one had ever meant enough for him to care that much. He didn't let anyone file any claims on him, and he didn't attempt to put any claims on them.

Who was her man? Could it be that young guy she'd been dancing with the night of the party? He'd even given up a trip to California to take over the wagon train. Surely that meant he was more than just a *friend.* Did he love Jamie? Even more important, did she love him?

Not that it mattered, of course. Matt just wondered.

She'd kissed him back in her sleep. Had she been dreaming about that guy? If she were any other woman, Matt's ego would have let him believe she'd been dreaming of him. But Jamie had convinced him there was no chance of that, as far as she was concerned.

There were moments—few and far between, but still moments—when he thought she didn't dislike him quite as much as she wanted him to believe. Sometimes her eyes lost that annoyed, distrusting glint they'd had since their first, rather strange meeting.

She shifted as if aware that someone was looking at her. Her lashes fluttered, then slowly opened until her gaze met his.

"Good morning," he said, not exactly pleased at the expression of panic that flickered across her features. She couldn't have acted more horrified if she'd awakened with a tarantula staring her in the face.

She scooted back to her side of the tent, moving with amazing quickness for someone wrapped in a thick sleeping bag.

"We overslept," she murmured, busying herself with putting her jeans on inside her bag. "I'll check on the horses, and you get breakfast started."

Before he could answer, she'd unfastened the tent flap and was gone.

Matt unzipped his sleeping bag and pulled on his jeans without haste. He felt as if he'd just survived a tornado, sweeping him into its center, spinning him around until he was dizzy, then spitting him back out.

By the time Jamie returned, he had bacon sizzling in the cast iron frying pan and a bowlful of eggs, scrambled and ready to pour into the grease.

She packed her toothbrush and other personal items into a small cosmetic bag, which she tucked into her saddle bag. She ducked into the tent and soon returned with her sleeping bag rolled and ready to be tied behind her saddle.

"I'll take over if you want to freshen up and get your things ready to pack," she offered, her composure back in full force.

He fished the bacon out and stretched it out on a paper towel, then poured the extra grease out. "Here are the eggs," he said, handing her the bowl. Their hands brushed as she took it, and Matt couldn't resist holding on just a few seconds longer than necessary. Jamie's gaze jerked up to meet his, and he gave her a slow, teasing grin. "Think you can handle it?"

She picked up on his double entendre and returned his smile with a renewed confidence. "There isn't anything I can't handle...if I choose to."

"Keep it warm for me until I get back," he added, releasing the bowl and stepping away.

By the time he returned, she had dished healthy portions onto their plates. He poured himself a cup of coffee, picked up his plate and perched on the edge of a downed log. Even after two days, his behind was too tender to sit any more than absolutely necessary.

"For some reason I wouldn't have guessed you could cook," he commented between bites.

"That's funny...I was thinking the same thing about you," she responded. "I'll bet Duke King can't scramble his own eggs."

Matt ran through his character's history. "Sure he can. He just chooses not to."

"Just as he chooses not to fall in love."

"That's because he's smart."

Jamie snorted. "No, that's because he's a coward."

"A coward! Duke has faced the toughest criminals in the Old West and never backed down."

"Yeah, I read about his lucky bullet." Jamie poured water in the frying pan and put it on the burner to heat. "He may be brave around a bandit, but he runs every time he gets close to a woman."

"Duke has gotten *very* close to quite a few women," Matt said, defending his hero.

"Physically... but never emotionally. Your Duke may be brave when he has a gun in his hand, but he's pretty weak when it comes to playing fair with the females."

"He doesn't lead them on. He tells them right up front that as soon as his business is finished, he'll be on his way out of town. But the women still throw themselves at him. They want whatever he has time to give them."

"That's a male fantasy if I ever heard one!"

"You don't think that's realistic?"

Jamie shrugged. "Oh, there are probably some women who would accept such treatment, but they're not the kind he would respect in the morning. I think you don't let Duke fall in love because you don't know how to handle the emotions." She tilted her head as she studied him. "I'll bet you've never truly been in love."

He opened his mouth to deny it, but he found himself saying, "Maybe not, but that doesn't mean I can't write about it. I've never shot a man, either, but that doesn't keep me from writing realistic action scenes."

"And you've never ridden a horse before, either," Jamie remarked positively.

Again he started to deny her accusation, then stood. Apparently, he hadn't been very successful in trying to hide his inexperience from her. "Okay, so I haven't ever ridden a horse. Big deal. I'm just a city kid. But ever since I was old enough to go to movies, I've loved Westerns. I think I've seen every Gary Cooper movie at least twenty times. And I read every book I could find on cowboys and gunslingers. I'll bet I know more about the Old West than ninety-five percent of the people who live smack in the middle of it.''

Instead of being impressed, Jamie's expression was sympathetic. "That's my point exactly. You've done your research, but you've never experienced the real thing. Then once you got into the saddle you found out it was a whole lot more difficult than you'd guessed." She looked directly into his eyes. "But until you've let yourself live it and feel it, you can't imagine what it's really like."

"That's why I'm here."

"So you'll leave Colorado knowing how it feels to spend days in a saddle and roughing it under the stars. But you still won't have a clue how to give Duke a heart."

Matt squeezed dishwashing soap into the pan of hot water and considered her comment as he washed his cup and eating utensils. "What do you suggest I do? Fall in love?" he asked, only half serious.

"As a matter of fact, I think it would be very good for you."

"No, thanks. I'm already in enough pain."

"Who says love has to hurt?"

"Everyone I know who's ever had the misfortune to actually feel the poison-dipped point of Cupid's arrow."

"You're such a cynic. No wonder Duke is a cold fish."

Matt washed their plates and flatware. "You sound like you're an expert on the subject of love. Is that guy from the dance the one who's taught you all about this hearts and flowers stuff?"

"Sam?" Jamie seemed surprised. "I'm not in love with Sam. He's just an old friend."

Matt was inordinately pleased to hear that. But still he pressed on. "If not Sam, then who?"

"No one. I'm still waiting for the right guy to come along. While you were busy reading about Wyatt Earp and Billy the Kid, I was reading about Rhett Butler and Heathcliff."

"The cartoon cat?"

Jamie dried the last fork and loaded everything into a heavy canvas bag with a noisy clatter. "You're hopeless."

No, he just wasn't a hopeless romantic.

He took down the tent while she saddled the horses and Maybelline. She helped him fold the heavy canvas and together they packed it on the mule's sturdy back. They worked well as a team and soon had the camp dismantled and the site cleaned.

Jamie mounted her horse and was securing Maybelline's rope behind her while Matt gathered Terminator's reins. Matt felt he and the horse had passed a point in their relationship. Matt viewed every minute he stayed in the saddle as cementing the bond between man and beast. Terminator had just been testing Matt, forcing him to pay attention. But now he knew he could relax and let the horse do all the work.

Matt grasped the saddle horn and was concentrating on sticking the long, pointy toe of his boot into the stirrup when Terminator stretched his neck around and clamped down on his rider's butt.

"Ouch! You stupid horse," Matt hissed, swatting backward to knock the animal's nose away. "Dammit, Terminator, we're the only males left on this trip and we're supposed to stick together. You are the or-neriest creature I've ever met." He twisted around so he could look at the wounded area, fully expecting to find a hole in his jeans. But the only thing visible from the outside was a ring of moisture where the teeth had touched the fabric.

The horse's nicker sounded very much like equine laughter.

Feeling totally betrayed, Matt mounted, keeping a tight rein and a careful watch on those vicious teeth. Jamie was already halfway across the park, so Matt, with a great deal of satisfaction, dug his heels into the horse's flanks. Terminator responded with a power-ful forward thrust that almost unseated his rider, but this time, Matt was ready with a tight grip on the sad-dle horn. It wouldn't win him any saddle-seat equita-tion classes, but it was very effective in keeping him on the horse's back.

Two hours later, after passing through a stretch of the thickest forest he'd seen and crossing over yet an-other switchback, Jamie pulled her horse to a stop at the top of a ridge. Matt rode up beside her and stood in his stirrups to relieve the double pain of his screaming muscles and aching rear.

Below them a large lake dominated the meadow. The water was so calm and smooth that it reflected the jagged mountain peaks behind it as perfectly as a mirror. Only a lone Canada goose drifted across the surface, leaving a fantail of ripples behind him.

"It's so clear," Matt commented, amazed not just by the clarity, but by the incredible blue-green color.

"That's the way water is supposed to be," Jamie said, then turned to look at Matt. "If you were to choose the campsite, where would you put it?"

He studied the topography, noting the uneven spots, the access to the water and the timberline. Finally he pointed to a flat area on the north side of the lake, just a few feet from a stand of aspens, whose branches were covered with the light green growth of new leaves.

"There, at the edge of those trees," he said.

Jamie nodded. "Good choice. We can use the trees to build a temporary corral for the animals and there will be plenty of wood for our campfire."

Matt took the credit for having considered all those things although they hadn't entered into his decision.

"Let's get the camp set up," Jamie continued. "I'm dying for a bath."

They unpacked and unsaddled the horses and Maybelline and hobbled them. Matt and Jamie gathered a couple of dozen long, straight trunks of downed aspen, then tied them to the upright trees about four feet off the ground to make a top rail. They repeated the procedure, adding a second rail about two feet off the ground. Matt watched with interest as she even fashioned one section into a gate with rope hinges.

Inside the enclosure, there was plenty of tall grass for the animals to eat and a trickle of a stream running across one corner to give them fresh water. Jamie and Matt rubbed their horses down, then Matt pitched the tent while Jamie finished with Maybelline.

When the camp was fully set up, Jamie took a towel, washcloth, soap and a change of clothes out of her saddlebags.

"I'll be at the lake," she informed him. "I'd appreciate some privacy."

What did she think he was...a peeping Tom? He was a grown man. He didn't have to sneak around, hiding in the bushes and spying on a woman while she took a bath. "I'll try to resist," he responded with a touch of sarcasm and turned his back to the lake to show how little it mattered to him.

But as he heard the sound of her splashing in the water, it took every ounce of his willpower not to glance around, hoping to catch the sight of her naked body. His mental image of her floating on her back on the glassy surface was almost enough to cause him to regress to a curious, oversexed teenager. Even worse, he was actually thinking how he could get closer without Jamie noticing him. The idea of the crystal-clear water trickling over her breasts and dripping off their rosy tips was more exciting than any *Playboy* centerfold he'd ever seen. He could picture her slender, athletic figure glistening in the sunlight as she ran the bar of soap over her skin. She would cup the water and pour it over her, rinsing the soap away in bubbling rivulets that would flow down, following her curves, slipping through the golden curls between her legs and...

"I feel a hundred percent better," she announced as she walked back into camp, fully dressed.

Matt whirled around, startled at her unexpected return and disappointed that he'd missed his opportunity to see if her bare beauty equaled his imagination. As he watched her bend her head sideways while she rubbed the ends of her hair with a towel, he noticed the shape of her breasts moving inside the sweatshirt.

Even though he couldn't see an inch of inappropriate flesh, it was obvious she wasn't wearing a bra. Suddenly, the thought of a cold bath seemed very appealing.

He ran his palm over the stubble of three days' growth of beard. He had decided not to shave during the entire trail ride. Sometimes, while he was wrapping up a book, pushing dangerously close to a deadline, he didn't eat regularly, didn't get more than a few hours' sleep per night and didn't waste time with the trivialities such as shaving and laundry. But even when he was wrapped deeply in a plot, he always found time for a daily shower.

"I think I'll take my turn now," he said as he dug through his duffle bag and pulled out a change of clothes and a towel. He began walking away, but tossed a parting shot over his shoulder. "Don't peek. I'd like a little privacy please."

Jamie gave him an amused look. "I'll try to resist," she echoed.

There was a growth of waist-high bushes near the water's edge that provided a perfect dressing area. Matt unbuttoned his shirt and took it off. He had to struggle with his boots, but they, too, were soon off to one side, followed by his jeans, socks and undershorts.

Close up, the water was even more beautiful. The surface sparkled like a bowl of diamonds, while, clearly visible in its depths, fish of all sizes swam lazily over the rocky bottom.

Matt loved water sports, especially sailing on Lake Michigan. He'd learned to scuba dive and sailboard in the Caribbean, and this mountain lake made him wish he'd brought his gear along.

Because of the incredible clarity of the water, it was impossible to tell how deep it was, so he decided against diving in. Instead he walked out to the edge of a flat rock that jutted over the lake. The sun felt good on his bare skin, and he paused for a moment. Overhead, a large bird glided in lazy circles. Although he'd never actually seen one flying in the wild, Matt knew by its white head and tail that it was a bald eagle. Awed by its beauty and power, Matt watched the bird float on the wind currents as he waited for an opportunity to catch something for his dinner. As his shadow passed across the lake, the fish would instantly vanish and wait for several seconds before daring to reappear. But one little trout wasn't quite quick enough as the bird swooped down with shocking speed and plucked the fish from the water.

It happened so fast that the water was barely disturbed. Only the circles rippling out from the center site and the wiggling fish gripped in the eagle's talons were the evidence that anything had happened. The fish would die so the bird would live, just one more link of the food chain.

Matt knew they wouldn't welcome his invasion of their territory, either, but he didn't want to wait any longer. Tucking his legs under him, he bounded off the rock and plummeted into the lake.

As the icy water closed around him, all the breath left his body. Desperate to get out, he pushed off the bottom and shot back up to the surface. Sputtering and gasping for air, he swam back to the big rock and pulled himself up on it, welcoming its heat.

He'd expected the water to be cold, but swimming under an iceberg couldn't have been any more frigid. He was surprised the fish were able to survive such temperatures. They must be fish sticks on the fin.

Matt glared at the water, then glanced toward the camp where he could see Jamie standing next to the corral, her back toward him. How had she been able to tolerate it so long? She'd bathed *and* washed her hair while he hadn't even been able to stay in for more than a few seconds.

Well, hell! If she could do it, then he could, too. Men were supposed to be tougher than women. He couldn't let her show him up.

But he could be smart about it.

His body and hair were already wet, so he lathered up while still on warm, dry land. Then, taking a deep, stabilizing breath, he plunged in one more time.

It didn't take him long to rinse and stagger out to where his towel was draped over the bushes. His teeth were chattering as he dried off and dressed in clean clothes. Then, drawing from his deepest masculine reserve, he arranged his features into his best nonchalant expression and even managed to whistle through his stiff, blue lips as he strolled back to camp.

Jamie was feeding logs onto a roaring campfire, and Matt sidled as close as possible to the radiating heat without being obvious about it.

"Have a nice bath?" Jamie asked, her bright eyes wide and innocent, alerting him that he'd been set up.

But he refused to give her the satisfaction. "Sure, it was great. I feel like I've lost ten pounds of trail dirt."

"It wasn't too cold for you, was it? It was probably still covered with ice up to a couple weeks ago."

"Nah, it was fine," he answered, inching closer to the fire.

Jamie shook her head in exasperation. "Liar! You're the most stubborn man I've ever met."

He glanced over at her as if he didn't have a clue what she was talking about. "Oh, did you think it was cold?"

"Of course I thought it was cold," she declared. "People have died from hypothermia in temperatures warmer than that lake."

"So why didn't you warn me?" he asked, watching for her reaction. If he expected her to be ashamed, she, as usual, surprised him with a dazzling smile.

"Because I thought it would be a good adventure for you. Just think of how many pioneers nearly froze their butts off in that lake."

Matt had had enough trouble resisting her when she was openly hostile toward him. But when she smiled like that with her lovely eyes twinkling and her delectable lips parted, he felt the breath whoosh out of his chest with the same force as when he'd jumped into the lake.

"Come on, tell the truth," she persisted. "That was the coldest water you've ever been in. And don't feed me any bull about men being able to take it. I think it's time you were honest with me and yourself. Admit it. You have feelings, too."

Matt was silent for a moment. He knew it was more complex an issue than it seemed. Just as the surface of the entire lake had eventually been disturbed by the ever-widening circles of one small disturbance, so would Matt's image be forever changed if he were to admit a weakness to this woman.

Maybe it was because he was surrounded by the honesty and purity of nature. Maybe it was because he was all caught up in the moment, with the emphasis on survival in the present rather than any reputation he might have earned in the past. Or maybe it was just because Jamie was so different from any other woman he'd ever met and because she was obviously not impressed with the self-confident stud he liked to have people think he was.

For whatever reason, Matt felt compelled to tell the truth.

Chapter Eleven

"It was like swimming in the Arctic Ocean. If I wasn't still so cold, I'd carry you back out there and toss you in," he said. "In fact, that would be a great way for me to warm up." He tossed his dirty clothes aside and darted around the campfire.

Jamie reacted quickly, whirling away from his outstretched hand. She faced him, dodging back and forth as he made a motion to move in one direction, then changed to the other. Finally, he lunged forward, barely missing the flames as he reached for her.

She was laughing as she ran across the meadow, barely able to keep out of his grasp. Several times she felt his fingers touch her, but a twist of her shoulders or a sudden turn kept him from getting a firm hold on her.

Feeling very pleased that she'd been able to outrun him, Jamie glanced back at him. But the teasing grin and his easy strides told her he was letting her escape.

He wouldn't dare actually throw her into the lake, would he? That would be a severe punishment for her, just because she hadn't warned him of the near-freezing temperature. It wasn't like she'd *forced* him to jump into the icy water.

But then, she'd treated him pretty badly since they'd first met. Not that he hadn't deserved it. There was something about his cocky self-confidence that had instantly made her feel uncomfortable around him. And yet there was something about that same cockiness and totally masculine attitude that had attracted her with the powerful strength of a bear to honey. Sure, the bear knows that where there's honey, there's bees, and that he'll probably get painfully stung. But the thought of the sweet, golden honey curling around his tongue and filling his belly made the reward worth the risk.

Was letting her guard down around Matt worth the risk? Would the attraction she was already feeling for him burn hotter or burn out? Was she a fool for letting the most exciting, best-looking man she'd ever met slip out of her life forever without really getting to know him?

Jamie had been rather satisfied with her life before she'd met him. The days had been predictable, but happy. Although there was no special man currently in the picture, Jamie had assumed that, sooner or later, the right guy would show up, probably buy a neighboring ranch, and together they would raise cattle and horses and lots of kids.

She'd never guessed a city slicker would breeze into town and throw her emotions into a turmoil. Not to mention the fact that she'd never felt such a strong, persistent physical desire for any man. All of a sudden her life seemed incredibly dull before he'd arrived.

And she didn't want to think about how quiet and boring it would be when he left.

Jamie dodged his hand again, but he must have tired of the game because, with a burst of speed, he caught up with her. His strength surprised her, but his laughing eyes kept her from being frightened. With little visible effort, even as she continued to struggle, he pulled her into his arms. But instead of carrying her to the lake, he began tickling her.

She'd been prepared to wrestle with him to keep from getting thrown in the lake. But his amazingly gentle fingers teasing the sensitive area around her rib cage took away all her resistance. Her feet stopped running, but the shift of her weight caught him by surprise. Together they teetered, then tumbled over.

His arms were wrapped around her, holding her, protecting her as they fell. He twisted so she landed on his body, cushioning her fall. However, as soon as they settled, he rolled over so she was pinned beneath him.

"I'm not letting you up until you tell me you're sorry," he said, grasping both of her wrists in one of his hands and holding them over her head.

She was laughing so hard, she could barely answer. "Sorry for what?"

"Sorry because you wrecked my car. Sorry because you didn't sympathize with me when I felt so miserable with altitude sickness. Sorry because you didn't dance with me at the party. Sorry because you made me ride a horse with the personality of a cranky grizzly bear." He paused for a minute, and his gaze focused on her lips. His voice was lower, huskier as he continued. "Sorry because you didn't admit you liked it when we kissed."

Jamie's mouth went dry. She'd been thinking up snappy responses for all his accusations until he'd added that last one.

"Come on, be honest," he taunted. "Let's play truth or dare. I admitted something to you. Now it's your turn."

"Okay, I'll admit it . . ." she hedged. As she looked up at him, staring into eyes the color of dark sapphires, her thoughts scattered. "I'm sorry...uh...that you and Terminator don't get along."

"That's an understatement," he snorted. "But that's not what I want to hear." He leaned closer and gave her a slow, sensual kiss. "Admit it."

"I can't say I'm sorry I wrecked your car, because that was all your fault."

His lips moved over hers again, gently, seductively. "Wrong answer. Try again."

She gulped, barely able to form an intelligent sentence as her blood began to race through her veins. "I didn't dance with you because you didn't ask."

He kissed her once more, nibbling at her lower lip as he leaned back. "I'll give you that one. But only if you promise to dance with me the very next time we have the chance."

Unable to speak around her heart, which seemed to have become lodged in her throat, she nodded.

He dropped light kisses on her eyes, her nose, her cheeks and finally her lips. "Say you like this . . ." he prompted, ". . . and this . . . and this."

"Why? To feed your ego?" she managed to ask. "Don't you have enough women begging for your kisses? Why do you need me to be added to the list?"

"I'm not keeping a list. And if I were, I wouldn't want you on it."

"I'm not sure how to take that."

"You're not like those other women."

"Yeah, right," Jamie retorted. "I'm just one of the boys."

Matt groaned. "No, you're definitely not one of the boys." He looked down at her with a sort of bewildered amazement. "I've known my share of women, but I honestly didn't care what they were feeling . . . emotionally, that is. All that mattered was that they and I were physically satisfied."

Jamie rolled her head to one side. "I don't want to hear about your physical prowess with other women."

"Good, because I don't want to talk about them. They aren't important."

Jamie turned back to study his eyes to measure his sincerity. "Don't try your lines on me. I don't play those kinds of games."

"That's just it!" he exclaimed. "With you I don't have to play games. You're not impressed with my career or my money or even my body." He grinned roguishly. "Although, I don't understand how you can resist such a perfect specimen. If you knew how many hours I spent in a gym to keep in shape . . ."

"Your body's not too bad," Jamie drawled, then added, "for a city boy."

"That's because you haven't seen it at its best."

"You want to bet?"

He pulled back and squinted down at her. "You didn't turn your back?"

Jamie hadn't meant for him to know she'd peeked while he was bathing. The sight of him standing on that rock, as beautifully naked as Adam in the Garden of Eden had frozen her in her tracks. For several minutes, she had shamelessly watched him, turning away only when she realized how embarrassing it would be for him to catch her, when she'd been so definite in her own bid for privacy. And now the truth had slipped out. It was not in Jamie's nature to lie, so even though she could feel hot spots of color rise to her cheekbones, she said, "Sooner or later I turned around."

A deep, warm chuckle vibrated from within him. "See anything you liked?"

"The eagle was beautiful." Jamie's embarrassment melted, replaced by a mischievous streak she couldn't resist. "No matter how many times I see one, I'm still impressed by their size and quickness."

"Quickness is not always a virtue," Matt commented wryly.

"Neither is size. I suppose what it all boils down to is skill and intent. How badly did he want that fish? Was it because he was really hungry or because he was just testing himself to see if he could catch it?"

Matt closed the distance between their lips. "He was starving," he whispered, his breath warm against her face. His mouth pressed against hers in a long, sweet kiss.

Then, before she could react, he pushed to his feet and held down his hand to help her up. Jamie brushed aside her disappointment and let him take her hand and pull her up. When he didn't immediately let it go, she met his gaze and felt her knees weaken from the open vulnerability she saw in those dark blue depths.

It was not an emotion she'd expected from this very independent man.

"I want you, Jamie, more than I've ever wanted any other woman. And it's scaring me to death." Matt brought her hand to his cheek and rubbed it against the roughness of his stubble in an oddly sensual gesture. "I thought all I wanted from you was to get you to bed. But somewhere along the line, that all changed. I want you to want me...I need you to need me. And I don't have a clue what to do next."

Jamie was genuinely touched by his admission. She sensed she was seeing a side of Matt Montana that few people had seen. But she didn't know what to do next, either. Anything that developed between them would be extremely short-term. Jamie could handle the passion as long it stayed short-term. The problem would be if she should fall in love with the man. She didn't want him to open up to her. The more she liked him, the more difficult it would be to let him go.

She decided to take the coward's way out by avoiding the issue entirely. Gently she pulled her hand away from his and said, "I think the very next thing we should do is to begin cooking dinner."

She tried to ignore the hurt in his eyes or the way the shutter dropped down again. Immediately the vulnerability was replaced by the now-familiar cocky macho grin.

"I cooked breakfast. It's your turn."

Jamie hated that she was responsible for the change in his attitude. Why was she so afraid of him? Or was she afraid of herself? Either way, the damage was done. She would never again get a glimpse of the real man behind the mask. And it was a shame, because that man was much more interesting and personable than the man facing her now.

This was all happening too fast. If only she'd had a little more time to consider her options, she wouldn't have panicked at the first sign of genuine sensitivity from a man who seemed to take great pride in being obnoxious.

"We've got some hamburger left," she said finally. "If it wouldn't offend your Italian sensibilities, I could make spaghetti with sauce from a mix."

Matt grimaced. "A mix! Oh no, I'm taking the cooking duty back and you get to wash the dishes. I'll grill us some hamburgers, okay?"

"Sounds good to me." Jamie knew she could stay and help, but the air was as tense and awkward as when they'd first met. Only this time, it was her fault. "I'm going to let the animals out to graze for a while," she said. "Do you know where everything is?"

He nodded, and she fled to the safety of the horses' company. She knew what to expect from them. Their demands on her were simple. There was responsibility, but little risk in owning an animal. Every day they required the same things—food, water, grooming and, to a lesser extent, affection. Jamie was comfortable with the predictable. What threw her off pace was the unexpected. And Matt Montana was nothing if not unexpected.

She snapped lead ropes to the animals' halters and led them to where the grass was the thickest. She hobbled their forelegs, then sat on a rock and watched them graze.

But her thoughts drifted off to other, more important subjects. She wondered how Dale was doing and how her father was feeling. She wondered if Boots, Lyle and Randy had made it out of the mountains without further mishap. She wondered how Sam was doing with the wagon train and if the mail had brought more reservations to fill the rest of the summer.

And she wondered why, even with so many other things to think about, she couldn't get Matt out of her mind.

By the time they sat down to dinner, a brisk wind had picked up, bringing thick, dark clouds with it.

"These are good," she told Matt after gobbling down a delicious hamburger as if she hadn't eaten in a week.

He flipped a couple more patties over on the grill, then scooped up one that had been cooking over the center flame. "Sorry about the bread, but we didn't have any buns. Want another one?"

"You go ahead and eat. I can fix my own."

"I'll do it. It'll be your turn tomorrow." He glanced over at her. "Unless you threaten me with spaghetti again."

She would have gotten up and done it herself in spite of his offer. But that would have meant more physical contact than she dared at the moment.

He handed her another hamburger, then made a couple for himself. As he ate, he studied the sky. "Do you think it's going to rain again?"

Jamie looked up. "Those look like snow clouds. We might get a few flakes before dawn."

"I guess we're heading back tomorrow."

"Yes," she answered.

He leaned against a tree trunk. "Too bad. I like it here. It's as if we're in a different world." He finished his second hamburger and wiped his mouth, then stood. "I'm going to take a walk," he said, and with his hands thrust into his jacket pockets, he moved away.

Jamie watched his stiff, straight back. His long legs covered the ground quickly until she could barely make out his silhouette against the dusky sky. Such a complex man. Jamie wished she could get to know him better. But they had so little time left.

HOW COULD HE have been so stupid? Whatever had possessed him to tell Jamie how he felt? Women didn't take that sort of information well. They either laughed or left. And Matt wasn't sure which hurt worse.

That wasn't true. He knew from experience that the hurt was much worse and lasted much longer when they left. Just as his mother had.

For years he'd wondered what he'd done to make his mother leave. Had he been so bad she couldn't stand to be around him? Had he been so much trouble she'd had to escape from his demands? Had he cried too much or whined too often? What would make a mother leave her five-year-old child?

Matt's father hadn't helped. He'd made no pretense of being pleased to be burdened with a young son. Many nights he'd come home drunk and had passed out on the couch. And then as Matt got older, there were the nights his father didn't come home at all. But somehow they'd managed to skirt the authorities. Matt wasn't sure if he was lucky or not to have avoided being turned in to Child Welfare. But no one had cared enough even to do that.

Matt had learned early how to cook because that was the only way he'd gotten to eat. An elderly neighbor had taken him under her wing, letting him hang around her apartment after school. She'd been the one to teach him how to cook and how to sew buttons on his shirts. And she had let him peck away on her ancient Remington typewriter.

Although Eva was old enough to be his grandmother, or possibly even his great-grandmother—Matt had never known her age—she began to take the place of his absentee mother. She'd held him in her lap and read him story after story, instilling in him a love for literature that would last the rest of his life.

But then, she too left. One afternoon when he was ten, he'd come home from school and found a coroner's car outside the apartment building. He'd run upstairs, but had pressed against the wall when the funeral home's gurney with Eva's covered body on it had rolled past. She'd died in her sleep, and, just like his mother, hadn't even said goodbye.

Her desertion had hurt almost as much as his mother's. He'd refused to go to her funeral. Even when Eva's daughter had come to visit Matt afterward, he'd refused to acknowledge his pain. He hadn't cried since his mother had left, when he'd vowed he would never cry again.

Eva's daughter had finally given up on getting through to the boy, but not before leaving a box of Eva's belongings for him, special things that Eva had thought he might like to have.

Matt had stuck the box in the back of his closet and not even looked inside until eight years later when he was about to go off to college. It was as close as he'd ever come to tears as he'd sorted through the books, including a couple of cookbooks, a few trinkets he'd admired as a child, a fringed pillow with an embroidered picture of the state of Texas, where Eva had been raised, and the old Remington typewriter.

A football scholarship and a full-time job after school and on weekends had paid his way as he'd earned a degree in history and business. He'd written every term paper and thesis on that manual typewriter, and eventually hammered out his first commercial short story. Before his college graduation, he'd sold his first Western adventure novel.

The typewriter had long since been replaced by a state-of-the-art computer, complete with hard drive and laser printer. But the Remington still had a place of honor on a shelf in one of his many bookcases. And he'd never forgotten the kindness of an old woman... or the pain of her unexpected departure, just as he'd never forgotten the absence of his mother's arms...or the anguish of her disappearance.

They were the only two women he'd ever loved. And they'd both left him. It wasn't worth the risk of loving... and losing again.

Chapter Twelve

Matt was standing on the rock that protruded over the lake when he noticed the weather was worsening. The wind whipped whitecaps onto the lake's surface and pushed a thick, opaque layer of clouds over the moon. Pine needles whispered a warning as dried leaves scuttled across the ground.

Maybelline gave a plaintive bray, drawing Matt's attention to the animals in the meadow behind him. Jamie was trying to hold the horses' ropes while she untied the hobbles, but the horses weren't cooperating. They were snorting and dancing around on their hind legs, while their shackled forelegs hopped and half reared.

Even though he didn't particularly like being around the horses even when they were in a good mood, Matt hurried over to help Jamie with the nervous animals. He took their ropes and used his weight and strength to hold their heads down while she quickly unfastened the hobbles. Maybelline was more cooperative, and soon Matt and Jamie were jogging toward their camp with the horses and the mule practically running over them in their eagerness to get back into the psychological safety of the corral.

Jamie had already banked the fire, completely burying the embers so a stray one wouldn't blow away and start a forest fire. Matt helped her suspend their food supplies from a tall branch, and they secured everything that might blow away, even bringing the items into the tent that couldn't be weighted down or would be damaged by bad weather.

A slushy frozen rain began to fall just as they finished, and Jamie and Matt dove into the warmth of their tent. Using a propane lantern for light, they worked together to rearrange things inside so there would be room for their sleeping bags. When everything was finally straightened, they plopped down on their sleeping bags and exchanged tired, but wary glances.

Jamie took a battery-operated weather band-radio from her saddlebags and tried to tune it in, but all she got was static.

"I guess we're too deep in the mountains," she said, finally giving up and turning it off.

"That wind felt like it was blowing in from Lake Michigan," Matt commented.

"I guess it made you homesick for Chicago."

"The wind is only one of the things I don't miss about Chicago."

"Have you ever lived anywhere else?"

"Just when I went to college, but even then I didn't go far, just across the lake to the University of Michigan."

"Do your parents still live in Chicago?"

Matt decided against going into detail about his father's death two years earlier and his mother's desertion twenty-seven years ago. "No, they don't," he stated flatly.

Jamie must have sensed his parents weren't a comfortable subject, because she didn't pursue it. Instead, she pulled out a deck of cards. "How about a game of gin rummy."

"Make it poker and you're on."

"Strip or penny?" she asked, sliding him a look he couldn't interpret from under the fan of her lashes.

Matt had given up trying to figure her out. She wasn't an open flirt like many women he came in contact with, but sometimes she popped out with something that was subtly provocative. She'd made it a point to let him know she was not inexperienced, and yet some of things she'd said made him doubt that she'd had very many romantic flings. Didn't she know she couldn't con a con? And Matt was a master at making people believe what he wanted them to believe.

But he wasn't in the mood to be set up again. If any moves were made, they would have to be made by Jamie. He reached into his saddlebag and pulled out a handful of change. As he'd dressed Monday morning, he'd automatically put it in his pocket—as if there was anyplace to spend it in the wilderness. After the first day, he'd left it in his saddlebag.

"Let's play for pennies," he said and was even more confused by her disappointed expression.

"I didn't bring any change with me," she admitted.

He refused to read anything into her words. "Here, you can have half of these," he said as he divided his coins into two piles.

Jamie shuffled, let him cut the cards, then dealt them out with a practiced efficiency. "Five-card stud, nothing's wild, Jacks or better to open."

Matt knew he was in trouble.

An hour later she had won all his money and was smiling triumphantly. Thank goodness they hadn't been playing strip or Matt would be freezing his bruises off.

"Where did you learn to play poker like that?" he asked.

"Long, cold winters with just my father and the ranch hands for company," she replied. "And they didn't want to play Clue or Trivial Pursuit."

"There are lots of better ways to spend long, cold winters than playing cards."

"Maybe in Chicago, but once it starts snowing we're pretty isolated on the ranch. We have to make our own entertainment."

"I can't believe there wasn't some lonesome cowboy who was more than willing to keep you warm and busy."

Jamie picked up a stack of coins and let them trickle onto the blanket with a muffled clink. "Oh, there've been plenty of lonesome cowboys drifting through the area. But they weren't what I was looking for."

Matt couldn't keep his gaze off her beautiful hair as the artificial light turned the golden strands to a spun silver. "So, what are you looking for?" he asked.

She sighed and leaned back against her saddle. "It's unrealistic, and sooner or later I'll probably have to lower my expectations, but I'm still waiting for my Prince Charming to come riding up on a white stallion and sweep me up on the saddle with him."

"And then you'd ride off into the sunset together?"

"I guess that's how all fantasies end, don't they?"

"Not mine." Matt chuckled. "After my experiences with Terminator, I'd rather sail off into the sunset."

"Are you still sore?"

He glanced at her sharply. "Sore? What makes you think I might be sore?"

Jamie's eyebrows arched in amusement. "Because you walked as if your undershorts had been starched and you never sat down when you were out of the saddle."

"You're determined to make me admit I'm a dude... and I don't mean that in the cool sense."

"I don't usually try to embarrass people, but you were so annoying. Besides, I honestly didn't know you weren't an experienced horseman. It sort of goes with the territory when you're in your profession."

"That's the problem. Other than a few trips to the library and bookstores, I didn't have to ride anything more lively than my desk chair. It's not something I wanted to announce to the fans of my books. I think they all assume that Duke King is my alter ego."

"Isn't he?"

Matt shrugged. "I suppose there's a lot of me in the character, but Duke is bigger than life, out there riding from town to town and righting wrongs..."

"And ravaging women."

"Well, that, too. But he never forces himself on them."

"He doesn't have to. All your female characters have been lobotomized. A woman might be irresistibly attracted to a man, but she must always have a choice of whether or not she wants to get sexually involved with him. With your women, it's a given. Have any of them ever said no?"

"Are we talking about the women in my books or the women in my life?" Matt joked.

Jamie shrugged, apparently taking him seriously. "Both."

Matt considered his response carefully. "I've heard a *no* or two in my life. But I don't suppose Duke ever has. Maybe I'll write one into my next book."

The wind howled around the tent, sucking the slack in the canvas walls and roof outward, then dropping it back with a pop.

"I think I'm going out to brush my teeth and check on the horses," Jamie said as she pulled on her coat and took her bag of toiletries out of her saddle bag.

"Need any help?"

"No, I'll just be gone a few minutes, then you can take your turn outside."

She unzipped the door, but before she could open it, the wind blasted inside, sending a swirl of snowflakes around her. She glanced over her shoulder and gave him a sheepish grin. "On second thought, I'd love to have your help."

"Sure," he answered and stuck his own toothbrush and paste into his coat pocket before pulling on his boots and following her out of the tent. She headed off to a thick undergrowth of bushes that had been unofficially designated as her private bathroom, several dozen feet away, and he went in the opposite direction toward the corral.

Fat, wet snowflakes plastered against his cheeks and dripped into his eyes as he crossed the short distance. He was wearing heavy gloves, but he could feel the cold through the layer of leather. He could just imagine how uncomfortable the animals must be.

The horses and the mule were crowded together with their tails to the wind and their heads lowered. The location of the corral behind a thicket of evergreens blocked the worst of the storm, but already a layer of snow blanketed them. Their breath puffed in clouds from their ice-coated nostrils.

Matt even felt a tinge of pity for Terminator... just a small tinge.

"I'm through. You can go now."

Matt looked down at Jamie who had joined him at the fence. The storm was so noisy, he hadn't heard her approach.

"Do you think they'll be okay out here?" he asked.

"What do you want to do...bring them into the tent with us?" she joked.

"The Arabs do. They take better care of their horses than of their servants."

"But they have huge tents. They can afford to be generous with their space." Her chuckle was almost lost in the wind. "Even though I love horses, I'm not sure I'd want to sleep with one."

"Who *would* you want to sleep with?" He'd meant the question to be a joke, but as their gazes met in the light of the lantern he was carrying, it became intensely provocative.

He could see the answer in her eyes, but even though her mouth opened, she didn't answer. Matt's heart did a happy dance in his chest. She wanted him. She could deny it all she wished, but now he knew. She wanted him as passionately as he wanted her.

Jamie dropped her gaze first and retied the knot that was holding the gate shut, even though the rope had been secure. He didn't press the issue because it would spook her like the doe they'd found on the trail or a wild filly edging closer for her first taste of sugar from an outstretched hand.

Good lord, he was starting to think like a cowboy. That would help his writing, but it could make him the laughingstock among his friends back in Chicago. Just imagine how they would react when he said *y'all* instead of *you guys* or talked about punching *dogies*. Actually, he wasn't too sure how that last phrase would ever work into a conversation.

Not that he had that many friends close enough to notice the difference. Matt kept to himself, except for rare occasions when he accepted invitations from acquaintances or worked out in the gym. He liked his privacy and being his own boss. It was nice to eat when he wanted, to sleep when he wanted, to leave his clean clothes on the couch if he didn't want to take time to fold them and to sprawl across his bed, hogging the covers when he slept. As much as he enjoyed women, he rarely let them spend the night. He simply didn't like waking up next to them in the morning.

"The horses will be fine," Jamie said, interrupting his thoughts. "They're used to bad weather. But I'm about to freeze."

"Here, take the lantern. I brought a flashlight," Matt told her. "I'll be along in a minute."

She nodded and hurried back to the tent.

Matt lifted the collar of his coat to keep the snow off his neck and zipped his leather jacket as high as it would go. He had to chip through the layer of ice that had formed on top of their drinking water even though only a few minutes had passed since Jamie had filled her glass. Quickly he brushed his teeth, then headed off to the area he'd chosen for his private functions.

He was on his way back to the tent when the beam of his flashlight reflected off two glowing spots on a limb ahead of him. Matt lifted the light until it shone on a round, prickly looking ball stuck on top of the limb. As he watched, the two spots reappeared, and he realized they were eyes and the ball was a creature. He didn't think it was an owl, it was too small to be a bear, and he didn't know whether possums lived in the mountains.

A gust of wind carried a handful of snowflakes down the front of his jacket, so Matt decided this was not the time for nature watching. He would ask Jamie about it later.

But nature had its own idea. As he took a step forward, the slick soles of his cowboy boots hit a patch of ice. He tried to catch his balance, but the more he struggled, the faster his feet slid until they skated wildly out from under him. His back slammed against the tree and, for an instant, stars swirled in front on his eyes as he slid down the trunk to the ground.

Before he could gather his wits, however, the vibrations of the tree dislodged its prickly occupant, sending it tumbling down on top of Matt.

Neither the porcupine nor Matt had time to react. Their meeting was unplanned and unwanted, and their separation quick as the porcupine rolled down his arm and waddled off, but not without leaving a trail of quills behind, embedded in Matt's leather jacket.

It took Matt a couple of minutes to steady himself enough to stand. The pain of the quills' points in his skin and the freezing temperature cleared his head enough for him to know he had to get back to the tent. Jamie could help him. He had to get to Jamie.

Jamie was already tucked into her sleeping bag with her coat rolled under her head when Matt ducked through the loose flap. Matt zipped shut the door, then turned around.

"What was going on out there?" she asked. "Loud cursing is not one of the typical night sounds of the forest."

"It is when there's a porcupine sitting on your shoulder."

"What?" Jamie sat up and moved the lantern closer to Matt. When she saw the scattering of quills protruding from the sleeve of his jacket, she gasped. "How did that happen? Porcupines don't attack unless they're annoyed or scared."

"I guess it would be safe to say he was both annoyed and scared. He was sort of knocked out of a tree on top of me."

He could tell she couldn't quite picture his description of the event, so he added, "It's difficult to explain. All I can say is that I hate cowboy boots. The damn things have my toes all crammed into points and they don't grip the ice worth diddly."

"I'll get the first-aid kit," she said, getting out of her sleeping bag without pausing to put her jeans back on. "We're going to have to take your jacket off very carefully. We don't want any of those quills to break off in your skin."

Matt eased himself down on his sleeping bag. The sight of her long, bare legs and her cute little bottom encased in pink panties did wonders to take his mind off his pain.

All too soon she located the first-aid kit and crawled over and knelt in front of him. He could have used a little more of her feminine anesthesia as she began easing the jacket off his shoulders.

"Be still," she insisted. "Try not to pull away."

A few more expletives escaped as she gently worked the barbs out of his skin with a sterilized needle.

"Actually, you're lucky more didn't make it through the leather and into your arm," she told him when she'd finally removed the jacket completely. Her fingers moved to the buttons of his shirt. Her manner was efficient and impersonal until she had his shirt completely unbuttoned. As she spread the panels apart, her hands suddenly stilled.

Her gaze fluttered across his bare, bronzed chest, then fled up to his eyes. "Your shirt has to come off so I can put medicine on the wounds," she explained, but her voice was strangely husky. "You wouldn't want any of them to get infected."

Matt couldn't resist a little smile. "Go ahead. I won't move. There might be some short quills left, you know."

The tip of Jamie's tongue circled her lips nervously, unaware of how titillating the gesture was. "I'll try to make this as painless as possible."

"You're doing a good job so far."

She had to lean forward in order to lift the material away from his shoulders. He could feel the warmth of her breath on his face as she concentrated on her task. Her fingers were soft as they slid over his skin.

His right arm hadn't been wounded, so he was able to slip it out easily. But she moved the sleeve down his left arm with much more caution.

"Can you lean toward the lantern while I check your arm?" she asked.

He complied, even though the motion brought him much too close to her. He could smell the fragrance of her shampoo as the crown of her hair tickled against his chin. The longer her fingers stroked his skin, the more he became aware of the heat that was settling in his loins. Slowly the pain was shifting to a more intimate part of his body.

"I don't see any more." She rocked back and pulled some cotton and alcohol out of the first-aid kit. "This might sting a little."

Matt nearly shot through the ceiling as she dabbed the alcohol on his wounds.

"Don't be such a baby," she chided.

"That's easy for you to say. You're not the one with holes in your arm."

"How long have you been so accident prone?"

He gave a wry snort. "Just since I sent off my reservation to the Rocky K Ranch. Not only did you send it back and it got lost in the mail, but I've been abused by my horse, attacked by a small woodland creature, my leather jacket's been ruined and I probably won't ever walk normally again. I've never felt so much rejection...and writers are very sensitive about that, you know.''

Jamie dotted his injuries with antiseptic cream, then sat back on her heels and studied her patient. Instead of the sympathy he expected, a muffled giggle slipped through her lips.

"Nurses are supposed to wipe their patient's brow and say encouraging things," Matt pointed out. "They're definitely not supposed to laugh."

Jamie tried to force the smile off her face, but without much success. "Poor baby, I'm sorry you got so many boo-boos."

"A little sincerity wouldn't hurt."

"I'm trying, but the image of a porcupine falling out of a tree and running down your arm is pretty funny."

Matt could feel his lips begin to twitch as he thought about what it must have looked like. "It wasn't very funny when it was happening."

"I think it's one of those things you'll be able to look back on and laugh."

"My whole Western experience is turning out to fall in that category."

"We promised to help you make memories that will last a lifetime. We didn't say if they'd be good or bad."

He grinned. "That all depends on whether I make it off this mountain alive and with all my toes."

"Well, gosh, if you put that sort of restrictions on me, I'm not sure I can deliver."

They laughed together, their eyes meeting in warm camaraderie. But the laughter stilled in their throats and their gazes locked in an intimacy that neither could deny. Matt could see an avalanche of emotions cross her features. But an open desire had replaced the disgust he had seen so many times before, and a breathless eagerness was now more evident than the cautious hesitation that had caused her to draw back every time he got close.

Neither seemed to make the first move, and yet somehow they were in each other's arms. Their lips met and all tentativeness was gone. Matt tried to hold on to his control, but when Jamie's fingers slid along his neck, burrowing into the thick hair at his nape, and her body pressed against him, he groaned and pulled her into his arms.

Her breasts, unbound and deliciously firm beneath her sweatshirt, were burning like hot coals into his chest. He wanted to see them, to feel their softness, to taste their sweetness. But he didn't want to move too quickly.

Her mouth opened slightly, inviting his tongue inside to dance and flirt with hers. Her hands trailed down his back, following the planes of his muscles in a sensuous caress. He rose to his knees to allow the fullness of their bodies to touch. As much as he tried to control his passion, he couldn't stop the rush of heated blood to his groin. She wouldn't be able to ignore the hardness of it digging into her tender flesh. If she was going to stop their lovemaking before it went any further, the evidence of his excitement should do the trick.

However, instead of moving away, she rubbed against him, rotating in slow, tantalizing circles. Did she know she was driving him insane? Was she really ready for the next step?

The irony of his caution was not lost on Matt. Being honorable or sensitive had never been one of his strong points. With any other woman he desired, he would have taken what she offered without question, without commitment, without hesitation. But with Jamie he wanted to protect her from being taken advantage of... even from himself. Maybe *especially* from himself. What did he have to offer her? He could give her a good time, a nice house, trips around the world and everything else money could buy. But she needed a man to love her unconditionally. And love was the one thing Matt knew nothing about.

With a willpower he didn't know he possessed, Matt took her by the shoulders and gently pushed her away. "Jamie, I don't think this is a good idea."

Even in the poor artificial lighting, he could see her cheeks flame. Her eyelashes dropped to hide her confusion, then lifted as she pinned him with her steady gaze.

"We're out in the middle of nowhere...all alone...a man and a woman with healthy sexual appetites and all of a sudden you have to get scruples?" Angrily she jerked her sweatshirt over her head and flung her arms wide. Wearing only those flimsy pink panties she leaned back on her heels. "What's the matter with me? I *am* a woman. I know this isn't the greatest body in the world, but do I have so little sex appeal that you won't make love to me even when I throw myself at you? Am I the only woman you've ever turned down?''

Even though her words were agitated, Matt could see she was deeply hurt by what she perceived to be his rejection—so hurt she was trying to lash back and hurt him. If it wouldn't have been totally inappropriate, he would have laughed out loud at the ridiculous turn of events. For once it was his good intentions that were getting him in trouble.

He had to reassure her that she was the most desirable woman he'd ever met, and he had to do it quickly. The exquisite sight of her perfectly proportioned body was testing his good intentions more than it was humanly possible to resist.

"You've got it all wrong, Jamie," he told her. "I'll admit I'm not a saint, but every once in a while I try to do something honorable... just to keep people guessing, I suppose. I was physically attracted to you practically from the moment we met. But you made it perfectly clear you weren't interested. I tried to ignore how my body reacts every time you're near me." He gave a wry, mirthless chuckle. "I can assure you that I've never once forgotten you are a woman... and I haven't for a minute not wanted to take you to bed."

Her modesty returned in a rush, and she crossed her arms over her bare breasts. "Then why...?" she began.

"Because somewhere along the line I stopped lusting after you and began caring about you. You aren't like the other women I've slept with. I'm a little ashamed to admit it, but they meant nothing more to me than a few hours' pleasure."

He reached out and took a lock of her golden hair and curled it around his finger. "Right now I want you so much my guts are tied into knots. But I don't want you to feel pressured or to do something you might regret in the morning." He heaved a shaky sigh. "Damn, being a nice guy is hard work."

Chapter Thirteen

To Matt's dismay, her eyes filled with tears and she turned away.

"Then I've made a fool of myself," she said in a small voice.

He felt as if his heart had been ripped out of his chest. He wanted to protect her, not humiliate her. Impulsively he put his arms around her and cradled her against his chest. "No Jamie, it's me who's been the jerk. I'm not a people person. I spend a lot of time alone... a lot more than you probably believe. When I make love to you... and I sincerely hope that happens very soon... it has to be because you want me for me. Not because I'm Matt Montana, world-famous writer. Not because I have some money in the bank. Not because, as you said, we're out in the middle of nowhere, all alone, with healthy sexual appetites. And not because I got hurt and you feel sorry for me. I have no difficulty seeing you as a beautiful, desirable woman, and I want you to see me as a regular guy."

She sniffled and looked up at him. Surrounded by a pool of unshed tears, her irises were a clear, pure blue, fathomless like the lake. "Yes, well, I have to take some of the blame. You and I didn't exactly meet on the best of terms. Even though I definitely noticed you were a man, you were so cocky and arrogant I didn't know how to deal with you. You threatened my hard-earned respect. For years I've worked so hard for people to treat me like one of the guys. Out here, it's a man's world and women are supposed to sew quilts and raise kids, not run ranches. But all of a sudden you showed up and reminded me just how much it hurts to be looked down upon by a guy with an attitude.''

"I didn't mean . . .''

She managed a weak smile. "Oh, you probably didn't even realize you were doing it. With men, power and respect come naturally. But women have to work for it. I was outraged that all you had to do was arrive and everyone was running around, treating you like a king.''

"Specifically, your father,'' he guessed.

Jamie nodded. "Yes, I suppose my father was one of the people who fawned the most.''

"And ever since your mother died, you've tried very hard to please your father, haven't you?''

"Well . . . yes, I have.''

"And it hurts when he doesn't notice you and appreciate your efforts, right?''

Jamie gave him a curious look. "How did you know that? Did my father tell you about me?''

"No, he didn't have to,'' Matt explained. "You and I grew up in different worlds, but we have one thing in common...our mothers weren't around when we were growing up, and our fathers didn't exactly take up the slack.''

"Your mother died, too?"

Matt felt his jaw automatically clench. He never talked about his mother. But he felt compelled to be honest with Jamie. "No, she didn't die. It would have been easier to get over losing her if she had." He swallowed around the lump that had risen in his throat.

"Where is she?"

"I have no idea. For all I know, she could be dead by now. But when she packed her bags and left while I was still asleep, she was very much alive."

Jamie reached up and caressed his stubbled cheek. "I'm so sorry. I was ten when my mother died, and I've missed her every single day since then. How old were you?"

Matt felt the unfamiliar sting of tears against his eyelids. "Five."

"Five! You were just a baby. How awful that must have been for you."

He tried a careless shrug, but his broad shoulders slumped. "I hear of people remembering the way their mother hugged them or how she smelled like roses or lilacs or something flowery. But I don't remember any of that. In fact, the only person I recall from my childhood was this old woman who lived next door. She was like the grandmother I never knew. It was with her that I began to love books. But then she died and I was on my own again."

"Where was your father through all this?"

"He was working a lot." Matt knew it was silly, but he had always been compelled to make excuses for the man who had sired him, then ignored him. Well, no more. It was time he faced the truth and told it like it really had been. "Actually, he was a bum. Yes, he had a job, but he also had some expensive habits like bars, bimbos and the ponies. He paid for the bare essentials such as food, electricity and the rent. But I don't have many more memories of him than I do my mother, and he lived with me off and on until he died two years ago."

Jamie's arms wrapped around his back and she gave him a big, warm hug. "At least my father was around, even if he never really forgave me for being a girl. Poor Matt, no wonder you don't know how to let people get close to you."

He realized she was probably right, but at the same time he'd never felt closer to anyone in his life. They'd been so wrapped up in the conversation, that it was only at that moment that he realized he was holding an almost naked woman, a woman he cared more about than anyone he'd ever known, a woman who was looking up at him expectantly, with the same realization dawning in her eyes. He smiled down at her.

"Funny you should use the word *close*." He spoke in a voice that had suddenly grown husky. "I don't think you and I could get much closer."

"No, we couldn't," she agreed. "But in fact, I will *never* let you make love to me."

Matt tried not to let his disappointment show. Just spending time with Jamie gave him more pleasure than being with anyone else. "I told you that I would be satisfied with a platonic relationship with you."

"Maybe you would be, but I wouldn't."

"But I thought you said . . ."

"What I said was I wouldn't let you make love *to* me." There was an undeniably sexy gleam sparkling in her blue eyes as she continued, "But I would let you make love *with* me."

For a man to whom words were his livelihood, he'd never realized there was a difference between those two terms in the context of lovemaking. And it wasn't that he was a selfish or inconsiderate lover. He was simply always the one in control. He initiated it and he finished it, when and where it was pleasurable to him.

But with Jamie he could see how it would all be different. He found her aggressiveness exciting and her flashes of innocence charming. Even more than his own satisfaction, he wanted their lovemaking to be the best she would ever have. They had only two more nights together, and he wanted to really make memories that would last them both a lifetime.

"I'm beginning to believe it doesn't matter if I make it out of these mountains alive," Matt murmured, his lips hovering over hers. "If I have to die, let it be in your arms."

He could feel Jamie smile. "And with your boots off."

"Among other things."

Slowly, he eased her down on his sleeping bag, following her. His kisses relayed all the passion that was raging within him. And hers responded with equal fervor. Their hands fumbled with the few remaining clothes they had on, her fingers whispering across the sensitive skin below his belly as she slid his zipper down, then pushed his jeans and underwear over his hips. His hands slipped inside her panties and caressed the length of her shapely legs, until he tossed the pink cotton briefs off to one side, then wiggled out of his own pants and shorts.

Jamie was waiting impatiently for him as he looked down at her, savoring the beauty and intensity of the moment. Slowly he lowered his body back onto hers, but his kisses started on the flat delicacy of her stomach and worked their way up. He was delayed for several minutes at the pointed peaks of her breasts, delighting as much in her passionate response to the caresses of his tongue and the suckling of his mouth as he did in the wonderfully feminine texture and fullness of her nipples. When he finally was able to tear his affections away from her beautiful chest and nibble a path along her neck to her ear, he knew they were both ready.

He took a moment to dig through his shaving kit until he found an old package of condoms he had stowed in there months ago. It was the one thing in his sex life he was adamant about. Other than the threat of disease, Matt was determined not to produce a baby. Just as he had nothing of value to offer Jamie, he felt he had even less to offer a child. The least he could do was offer Jamie that protection.

As he pressed against the small, intimate doorway to her feminine core, he hesitated again. He was so hard and swollen, he was afraid he would hurt her. But Jamie's hands stroked down the curve of his back until her palms flattened over the muscled flesh of his buttocks.

"Yes, Matt. I want you as much as you want me... and I need you." Her fingers tightened and she urged him to enter her.

It was a tight fit, but her warmth and her wetness welcomed him. This was where he belonged. Her hips lifted, thrusting against him as he moved inside her, smoothly and slowly at first. As their heart rates quickened, joining in perfectly matched beats, his momentum increased. Even though only moments had passed, he felt as if he was about to explode. Never had his restraint been so sorely tested.

When he felt Jamie's nails dig into his buttocks and heard the sharp intake of her breath, he knew he wouldn't have to hold back much longer. For an instant there was a look of incredulity in her eyes before her eyelashes squeezed shut, clinging to the spasms of passion that rippled through her body.

Her muscles tightened, pulling his satisfaction from deep within him. Matt moaned with a pleasure so pure he almost lost consciousness as he gave one last thrust and pumped his heat inside her, joining her in ecstasy.

He collapsed on Jamie, trying to keep his weight to the side so he wouldn't crush her. He barely had the strength to breathe, much less support himself over her. But what he wanted most was not to break the connection that bonded them, permanently and intimately.

However, a stray gust of cold wind curled around their naked bodies, bringing them both abruptly back to reality.

Matt gave Jamie one more long, lingering kiss, then reluctantly crawled to the doorway. He unzipped the flap enough for him to peek outside.

"It looks like it's getting worse," he said, refastening the flap after a cloud of snow pushed its way inside. "Maybe you should call your father and get a weather report."

"Good idea," Jamie agreed. She pulled her sweat-shirt on, then pulled the radio out of the pack. It took several minutes to finally get through to someone, and even then the signal didn't carry all the way to the ranch, but was intercepted by a radio operator in be-tween. He gave them the report that a low pressure system had stalled and they were predicting up to a foot of snow overnight.

Jamie was distracted by Matt as he tried to block all the places where the cold air might leak through. Gloriously naked, his well-proportioned body could have passed for a Michelangelo statue. Beneath the bronzed skin of his broad shoulders, the muscles bunched and rippled as he stacked their saddle blan-kets against the edges of the zipper as double insula-tion. His torso tapered down to where his tan line stopped and his pale, chiseled buttocks tightened as he moved.

Pale except for the very vivid, odd-shaped bruise, a bruise that looked very suspiciously like teeth marks.

"Can I pass a message along for you, Jamie?" the man on the radio asked. "Over."

"Yes, would you contact my father and tell him we're not going to begin our trip down until the con-ditions are right," Jamie told him. "We have a secure camp and enough supplies." Matt glanced at her over his shoulder and gave her a smile so sexy that she felt her insides begin to melt again. "And tell him not to worry. We're keeping warm," she added. "Over."

She signed off the radio and returned it to her pack. "It looks like we're going to be stuck here a couple of extra days."

He shook his head and threw up his hands. "Darn, that's just awful." He crawled back to her on his hands and knees until he was only a few inches in front of her. "But I'm sure we'll find something to do to keep us entertained."

"I think the first thing that would entertain me would be for you to tell me how you got a bite mark on your butt."

Matt twisted around until he saw the dark purple bruise. "That stupid horse tried to take a chunk out of me. What do you feed that thing, human flesh?"

"Terminator did that?"

Matt seemed surprised that she would even have to ask. "Who else? Look at the size of those teeth. I've dated some unattractive women, but none of them had choppers like that."

He leaned forward and caught Jamie's lips in an unexpected kiss. "Do I detect a note of jealousy?"

Jamie started to deny it, then shrugged. "Okay, so I'm not too thrilled at the idea of someone else biting you anywhere, much less on your buns. At least not while I'm sort of responsible for you."

"You're going to take care of me, huh?" He wiggled his dark eyebrows roguishly.

"I'll do the best I can. But, frankly, you're proving to be quite a challenge. I can't protect you from every furry little animal out there."

"You can if we never leave this tent."

"We'll starve to death."

He slid his hands under her shirt and cupped her breasts in his palms. "Ahh, but what a wonderful way to go."

"And it would probably make your books sell through the roof, wouldn't it? I can see it now in the tabloids. Famous Author Died in the Arms of an Unknown Woman on Top of the Continental Divide."

His eyes twinkled. "It would probably put me on the *New York Times* bestseller list."

"Yeah, and it would put the Rocky K out of business."

"Okay, so we won't die. But we could build a log cabin and homestead this land, just like the pioneers. I'll catch fish and you can make our clothes out of deerskins."

"Isn't that just like a man!" Jamie declared with amused indignation. "You're out fishing while I'm busy working. I hate to sew."

"Fine. Then you can fish with me and we'll go naked." He slipped the sweatshirt off her head. "This could be our Garden of Eden, our paradise."

Jamie shivered. "I don't know about you, but this is not the sort of weather to be talking about becoming nudists."

"Care to share my sleeping bag? I'll keep you warm."

"These sleeping bags weren't designed for the kind of warmth-generation system you have in mind. But," she said, taking her bag and opening it, "we can zip them together and we'll have plenty of room."

"You sound like your bag's been double-zipped before."

Jamie couldn't resist a teasing smile. "Do I detect a note of jealousy?" she asked, echoing his question.

"Okay, so I'm not too thrilled at the thought of someone else sharing your sleeping bag."

"I think it's an easy bet that my sleeping bag's seen a lot less action than yours has."

Matt gave her a mischievous wink. "And that's the way it should be because I'm a..."

"A macho jerk," she finished for him. "Why should it be acceptable for men to sleep with dozens of women when women should save themselves for that one special guy? That's not fair."

"So you think a guy should confine his affections to just one woman... forever?"

"Yes, I do. If he loves her enough, he won't mind."

Matt's expression sobered as he stared into her eyes. "You know, I think you could be right." He followed her lead and unzipped his bag.

Jamie was beginning to understand why this man had never been able to make a commitment. No one had ever made a commitment to him. He had no role models or personal experiences on which to base his relationships. It would take a person who was patient enough to teach him. And it would take a person who loved him enough to wait until he learned how to love and how to let someone love him. As Jamie looked at Matt, her heart swelled with the rush of feelings he generated. Yes, she could be that person.

She'd tried so hard to resist him. His reference to the Garden of Eden had been particularly appropriate considering he'd dangled that tempting apple in front of her once too often. Especially since that soured romance, it had been a personal policy of hers not to get romantically involved with the guests. She didn't want to be a cowgirl version of Julie from *The Love Boat*, having a different boyfriend every week and always being left behind when he returned to his real life.

And Matt, of all people, had been the least likely candidate. There were a couple of times she would have been delighted to chase him with a cocked pistol all the way back to Chicago. But he had turned the tables somehow. There was no logical reason for it, but she'd actually begun to like the guy. And then, since her hormones betrayed her by being wildly attracted to him, she should have known it was hopeless to fight it.

Once in his arms, she'd wished she hadn't kept that wall up for so long. It was wrong and it was foolish. But for the next few days, he was hers. He would never know how tempting it had been when he'd jokingly suggested setting up residence right here in the meadow. At least for a little while longer, she could talk with him, laugh with him and make love with him as if their sleeping bags would be zipped together forever.

They snuggled into the double-size bag and Matt stretched up to turn off the valve of the lantern. As the light slowly faded, he took her into his arms again.

"I guess we really should try to get some sleep," he said with a notable lack of enthusiasm.

Jamie pulled his face down to hers and she gave him a kiss filled with all the desire and frustration she was feeling. She knew it was silly to spend what little time they had left together moping about when she wouldn't be able to run her fingers through his thick, gorgeous hair or kiss his wonderful lips or feel his boldness pulse within her. Even his almost-four-day-old beard was beginning to soften slightly, providing a stimulating friction against her tender skin.

"We can sleep next week," she murmured. *And next month and next year,* she added to herself. Right now she was in paradise.

Chapter Fourteen

"You're determined to kill me one way or another, aren't you?" Matt moaned, but there was no hint of remorse in his dark blue eyes. "I may never walk normally again."

"Are you still complaining about saddle sores?"

Matt stroked his hand along the curve of her hip, dipping in to her waistline, then along her rib cage as she lay on her side facing him. "No, I was referring to a different and much more rewarding exercise."

Jamie stretched her legs. She, too, was feeling the effects of a night filled with lovemaking, but she wouldn't dare admit it to Matt. "Why are men such babies? They simply can't take a little pain without complaining about it to whoever will listen."

"That's easy for you to say! You don't have a bite bruise on your rear and matching black and blue marks on your thighs from an attack horse, or dozens of porcupine holes in your arm."

"While we're comparing bruises, look what your horse did to me." She flipped over to her other side and pulled her hair away to reveal the large yellowish-green mark that covered most of her left shoulder.

"*My* horse?"

"Your Mustang. That's the bruise I got when I bounced across the hood of your car."

He leaned forward and tenderly planted a circle of kisses on her bruise. "I apologize for my horse. I had no idea he hurt you so badly."

"And I apologize for *my* horse," Jamie echoed. "If I'd known you weren't an experienced rider I would have given you a more docile animal." She thought back to her very poor first impression of Matt and shrugged. "No, even if I had known, I probably still would have given you Terminator, because the two of you have very similar personalities."

Matt whipped the top sleeping bag down and playfully sank his teeth into her soft buttocks.

"Ouch! What are you doing?" she gasped, rolling away from him.

He neighed and shook his head.

"See what I mean?" Jamie rearranged his dark hair where it fell across his forehead, until it was like a horse's forelock. "Whoa, my beautiful Italian stallion. One more trick like that and I'll put you out with the other horses."

He nudged her neck with his nose and nibbled the sensitive skin behind her ear.

Shivers streaked through her, starting at the place where his teeth teased her neck and radiating down her body. She'd made love more times last night than all of her previous experiences combined. But that, too, she dared not tell Matt. She didn't want to make him think he had too much of an advantage in the sexual expertise department. All night they had been like honeymooners, making love, sharing secrets and sleeping only when totally exhausted.

But as much as Jamie wanted to stay and let him nibble his way down to other sensitive areas, she had other responsibilities.

"Speaking of horses, I've got to go check on ours."

"Right this minute?"

"If I don't leave now, I'll be here for at least another hour. Besides, nature's calling."

"Be careful of the ice. I don't want to have to pick porcupine quills out of your pretty, already wounded shoulder."

With a great show of reluctance, he got up and dressed while she did. But when he picked up his jacket he groaned aloud at the sight of the quills piercing the expensive leather.

"It looks like a bovine pin cushion. What with the rain, the snow, the rocks, using it for a pillow and now this, I think it's ruined," he commented sadly.

"Actually, porcupine quills are quite fashionable out West. The Indians used them to decorate their leather clothing," Jamie told him. "However, they sewed them on top rather than sticking them in like you did."

"Smart aleck!" Matt flashed her an affectionate grin. "Just for that, I'm going to let you help me pick those suckers out later. And I'm going to go outside without a jacket and probably catch pneumonia."

"Then I'll have to nurse you back to health," Jamie promised with a sexy wink.

"Keep it up woman, and those horses will just have to fend for themselves."

A light snow was still falling. The thick layer of clouds refused to let the sun peek through, so it was difficult to tell what time of day it was. Not that it mattered to Jamie, because she wouldn't have been unhappy if time could somehow stand still.

After taking care of their personal hygiene, Jamie and Matt lowered the sack of food and took out the animals' bag of oats. Jamie cleared three patches in the snow inside the corral and poured a measure of grain onto the grass in each. Matt started a fire and began cooking breakfast while Jamie watched the animals eat, keeping the more aggressive Terminator from stealing food from Stormy and Maybelline.

By the time the animals had finished their breakfast, Jamie was starving for hers. She hadn't realized how hungry she was until she smelled the bacon and eggs cooking.

"If you ever get tired of writing and want to take up wrangling, we could always use a good trail cook," Jamie commented as she loaded her plate.

"Yeah, and I have such a way with horses." Matt gave her a wry smile. "If you let me ride a four-wheeler instead, I'll consider your offer."

"Would Duke King trade in his horse for a four-wheeler?"

"No, but he wouldn't be cooking breakfast when there was a woman around, either."

Jamie gave him a pointed look.

"Okay, so Duke King is a little bit too macho for the nineties," Matt conceded. "But he has to be true to his era in certain ways and bigger than life in others."

"A *little* too macho? His picture is probably next to the word *macho* in the dictionary." Jamie studied

Matt with a new perspective. "And up to a couple days ago, I would have said your picture would be right there, too."

"I haven't changed."

"No?" Jamie didn't agree, but she didn't argue. In her opinion the man sitting on the log across from her was, in many ways, very different from the one she'd originally met. "Well, maybe you and I are just looking at things differently than we were. At first I thought you and Duke were flip sides of the same coin. But now, here you are, cooking and helping with the camp chores."

"I told you I cook for myself all the time."

"Yes, but you're cooking for me."

He paused for a few seconds as if thinking of a snappy response. But what he finally said was, "Why not? I can't let you do everything."

It was not exactly the answer she wanted. Jamie wished he'd said it was because she was special and that she meant something to him. It wasn't like he was serving her caviar and champagne. Not that that would be her choice of a fancy meal. But bacon and eggs weren't exactly the most meaningful foods to be served.

The snowflakes fell into the fire and dotted the frying pan before melting with a sizzle. The weather seemed determined to chase Matt and Jamie back inside the tent.

Jamie raked her fingers through her hair. "I don't know about you, but I'm getting pretty wet."

"Take our plates in and I'll put the food away," he said, not waiting for her answer before he began gathering up the supplies.

She accepted his offer and made two trips to the tent, carrying the food, their cups and the coffeepot. She tried to shake off as much snow as possible before going inside, then took off her coat and hung it from the center pole near the doorway so it wouldn't drip on the sleeping bags.

Looking at the zipped-together bag, a wave of belated shyness swept over Jamie as she remembered all that had happened between those insulated shells. She had never given herself so freely and so enthusiastically to anyone, including the only other man with whom she'd shared a bed.

Jamie glanced at Matt's prickly leather jacket and chuckled. He was such a contradiction. Outside, he was all swagger and bravado, but he'd shown her that underneath that aggressive attitude, he was sweet and very tender. After being with Matt, Jamie couldn't imagine she would ever be satisfied with anyone else.

The thought of the other women who had felt the pleasure of his caresses and the heat of his passion was enough to drive Jamie crazy. How many had there been? He had told her he'd never been in love before and that none of his dates had ever meant anything to him. He'd said she was different. But could he ever fall in love with her?

A resigned sigh escaped Jamie's lips and she sank onto the rumpled sleeping bags. The fact that she cared about the other women in his life set off an alarm bell clanging in her head. The fact that she should want him to fall in love with her made those bells sound like the security system on Liz Taylor's jewelry vault.

She shouldn't care. She had no reason to want his love. No reason at all . . . unless you counted one little bitty complication. Jamie had fallen in love with him.

It simply wasn't possible. She couldn't have fallen in love with a man like Matt.

A man like Matt? A man who had been betrayed by everyone he'd ever loved. A man with a gentle heart and a quick, witty intelligence. A man who had the body of a movie star and the soulful eyes of a lost boy. A man who could make her laugh and make her cry. And she was sure to do plenty of the latter once he tired of her and went back to his city girlfriends.

Jamie straightened the sleeping bags and tidied up the small room. Obviously, she had only two choices. She could either shut all systems down, unzip the bags and force the wall back between them so the separation wouldn't be quite so painful. Or she could love him with all her heart, soul and body while they were together and deal with getting over him later.

Jamie, being the lover of romantic literature that she was, chose the Scarlett O'Hara solution and decided she would deal with it tomorrow. Today . . . and to-night . . . she would love Matt as if there was no to-morrow.

"I think it's letting up a little," Matt said as he backed into the tent, shaking off the snow and re-moving his boots before he reached the sleeping bags.

"Then we'll probably be able to get started back down sometime tomorrow."

Matt gave her a wryly innocent look over his shoul-der. "Did I say *letting up?* I meant really *coming down.* Boy, I've never seen such a blizzard. The trails probably won't begin thawing for at least a week."

"Good try." Jamie's smile was bittersweet. "But we're going to have to leave here no later than day after tomorrow. I've got to get back to the ranch. My father won't be able to handle checking in the next group and getting them settled. And we have a local rodeo scheduled for next Tuesday."

Matt sat down across from her and poured himself a cup of coffee. "What makes you think your father can't handle them?"

"Dad's great with the stories and providing the color. But he's not good with the business end or keeping things organized."

"I thought you said he took you for granted," Matt commented, referring to one of their lengthy conversations about their parents. "Maybe this is your chance for him to realize how much he needs you."

"I know he loves me, but he's just an old cowboy, a lot like your Duke. Even if he realized he needed me, he wouldn't admit it."

"What if I told you *I* needed you?" Matt kept his tone light, but his eyes never left hers as he asked, "What if I were to ask you to let your father handle his own ranch and for you to pack your bags and go to Chicago with me?"

Jamie was surprised at his suggestion, but because she didn't want to read more into it than was intended, she inquired, "Is this a hypothetical question . . . or a proposal?"

Now it was Matt's turn to look surprised. "It's definitely not a proposal. I'm not ready for marriage." He shrugged. "In fact, I'm not sure if I'll *ever* be ready for marriage."

"Then, as a hypothetical question, I'd have to give you a hypothetical answer and say I can't see myself ever leaving the ranch, especially for an apartment in the city. I'm afraid it'd be incredibly claustrophobic. I can't imagine not having the wide, open spaces and the Rocky Mountains outside my windows." She pushed the cold scrambled eggs around on her plate, no longer interested in eating. "Besides," she added, trying to pretend the conversation wasn't breaking her heart, "where would I keep Stormy?"

"I could rent another space in the parking garage."

"What about Terminator?"

"We have a dog food factory nearby."

"Matt!"

Matt called loudly, as if the horse could hear, "Just joking, Terminator, old buddy, old pal. I'm still waiting for us guys to bond."

"He's a gelding, remember? His loyalties are more with the person who feeds him. Sex or gender is no longer a big factor in his life."

"Poor guy," Matt said, genuinely sympathetic. "No wonder he's always cranky."

"Finish your breakfast," Jamie told him. "I feel like beating you again."

Matt's eyes wiggled up and down suggestively.

"At poker, you idiot," Jamie quickly clarified.

"But I don't have any change left."

Jamie's gaze moved slowly over his body. "Maybe we can increase the stakes." She laughed at the interested twinkle that leapt into his midnight blue eyes. "I was thinking about the royalties on your next book."

Matt set his plate aside and gave her a dangerous grin. "I might not have a next book. I'm seriously considering that trail cook job . . . as long as you and I can share a tent.''

Jamie handed him the deck of cards. ''Deal and we'll talk later about major changes in your life.''

NOT ONLY did the snow stop later that afternoon, but the sun finally burned through the clouds and began the melting process. After a couple of hands of totally crooked poker, including a very pleasurable awards ceremony where the loser, Jamie, gave the winner, Matt, a massage that ended up with neither of them really losing, they spent an hour picking quills out of his jacket.

''I don't know about you, but I feel like getting out,'' Jamie said. ''I need some exercise.''

Matt stretched, not anxious to leave the warmth and comfort of their canvas home. For a man accustomed to going to the gym almost every day, he was enjoying being lazy. ''Exercise? I can barely move and you're wanting to go out and tromp through the snow.''

''No, actually, I was thinking about taking the horses out. They haven't been as active as we have.''

Matt couldn't let her outdo him, even though the last thing he wanted to do at the moment was spend time with Terminator.

The horses were frisky and delighted to get out of their small corral. Matt was glad the snow was deep enough that they couldn't bounce around too much. He would have thought a day off would have given his aches time to heal. But the muscles inside his thighs were even stiffer and more painful than the first day.

Of course, his extracurricular activities hadn't exactly let those muscles rest. It proved he'd gone too long since he'd last made love . . . or had it really been just sex as Jamie and he had discussed? There was no denying it was different with her than it had been with any other female companion. And now that he knew how special it could be, he wasn't all that enthusiastic about going back to merely satisfactory.

Jamie would be a hard act to follow. Where would he have to go to meet someone like her in Chicago? There was nothing of quality in the singles bars. He knew all the women at the health club and none of them measured up to Jamie, in more ways than just their physical abilities. He didn't work outside his home, so that eliminated meeting a woman in his work place. It was too bad there weren't more "Jamies" out there so everyone could have one.

Actually, he couldn't believe his good luck to have the one and only Jamie. What was wrong with the guys in Colorado, anyway? Why hadn't someone already staked his claim and given her her own ranch and a houseful of babies?

But the thought of her married and pregnant with some cowboy's kid was enough to make him nauseous. Some other guy would be feeling her firm, lithe body pressed against his. He would be the one making her soft, beautiful lips curve into that slow, drawling smile Matt had come to look forward to seeing. Some other guy would be able to caress her breasts and bury himself inside her warmth.

They reached the top of a small, bare knoll and Jamie reined in her horse. The snow was as pure as milk and sparkled like crushed diamonds in the sunlight. The trees were liberally dusted, their limbs weighted down with mounds of accumulated snow-flakes.

"Isn't it beautiful," Jamie said with a contented sigh.

But Matt's attention was not focused on the scenery. Instead, he couldn't drag his gaze away from her proud, perky profile. He had become so familiar with each of her strong, beautiful features, he could visualize them even with his eyes shut. However he stared at her now, etching them even more deeply into his memory. It was odd, but she was the first woman he wanted to remember.

Would she remember him? Would she miss him... even a little? It came as quite a shock for Matt to realize how much he hoped she would. He didn't want to think that what they had shared in the last few days, whether it was their spirited bantering or their equally spirited lovemaking, would not be special enough for her to cherish forever. Surely she wouldn't be able to replace him in her thoughts and in her bed without at least a touch of wistfulness. He knew she wouldn't be easily replaced in his.

Jamie glanced over at him and her eyes were sparkling with a joy for life. A cool breeze skipped over the snow and whispered through her long, saffron-colored hair, lifting it and letting the strands trickle down as if human hands were playing with it.

If Matt were ever to father a child, he would want it to look exactly like Jamie.

A baby! Matt nearly slid off Terminator's back. How had a baby sneaked into his thoughts? He'd vowed *never* to be responsible for bringing a baby into the world. And he'd never been tempted to change his mind. But suddenly he was considering the possibility... with Jamie.

It was crazy. It was impossible. It was...

He hesitated. Could it be love?

He had nothing to which he could compare this change of heart. But he knew he'd never felt like this before. Matt had also never felt at such a loss. What should he do next? Confess his feelings? No, until he knew what they were, shouldn't he keep quiet? Ask her how she felt? Not that, either, because he knew it would hurt even worse than his mother's desertion if Jamie didn't have similar feelings for him. Or should he just try to forget about the whole thing? Maybe once his hormones quieted down, his sanity would return.

"Doesn't this inspire you?" Jamie asked, interrupting his rambling thoughts.

The question caught him off balance and he tried to get back into the conversation. "Inspire me?" he repeated.

"Yes, all this wild, unmarred beauty." Her arm swept in an all-encompassing gesture around them. "This is exactly as it looked to the first explorer who topped this ridge. This should be very helpful when you're writing your books."

"My book!" he echoed, knowing he was beginning to sound like a parrot, repeating everything Jamie said. "I have a book due in a month, and I haven't written one salvageable word." He'd forgotten all about it. He'd been so busy acting like a horny teenager that he'd pushed aside all thoughts of his book.

"Can you make your deadline?"

He shook his head. "I don't know. I've really gotten behind on this one. I'll have to dig in and work extra hard to get it done."

Her expression grew solemn. "Then we'd better hurry back so you can get to work."

Chapter Fifteen

It felt good to sleep in her own bed again. As much as she enjoyed the outdoors, after a week of sleeping on the ground, the cushion of a mattress beneath her was quite a luxury.

But the bed seemed way too large. It was the same bed she'd slept in since she'd outgrown her crib twenty-seven years ago, and yet she'd never noticed how big and empty it was.

She turned over onto her stomach and stretched her legs diagonally across the bed and spread her arms wide. It was nice to have all that space to herself. She'd been so cramped in that sleeping bag, even when the two were zipped together.

Who was she trying to fool? It wasn't the bed; it was Matt. In only five nights she'd grown so used to feeling his body next to hers that she felt lost without him.

Jamie rolled onto her back and stared at the ceiling. Outside her window an ancient cottonwood tree rustled in the night wind. The moon, edging toward fullness, silhouetted the large leaves, making abstract patterns that danced and played on the walls and ceiling.

Her window was open, letting in the cool, fresh air. The snow hadn't reached below ten thousand feet elevation, so none had fallen on the ranch. And now, even the snow in the mountains was almost gone, melting quickly under the warm June sun. She and Matt had had no difficulty following the trails out of the mountains. Their worse inconvenience had been the muddy paths. Matt and Jamie had had to take spot baths before they dared get into their sleeping bags during the three nights it took to get back to the ranch.

It had felt good to take a long, hot, tub bath and wash the trail dirt off her body and out of her hair. However, it had also served to take away the subtle scent of Matt that had clung to her. There were many things about the trip that weren't worth remembering. But Matt's tender touch, Matt's masculine scent, Matt's hard athletic body, Matt's sharp, irreverent tongue all were very much worth holding onto in her memories. In fact, they would be long cherished as the best thing that had ever happened to Jamie.

And oh, how she wished the world had not intruded on their happiness and forced them back home. With an exasperated sigh, Jamie flopped back onto her stomach and squeezed her eyes shut.

MATT POUNDED his pillow into a different shape and tried to fit it comfortably beneath his head. He kicked off the covers and moved around, hoping to find a good position that would be conducive to sleep. After getting so little sleep during the past week, he would have thought he'd drop right off as soon as he laid down. Instead, his muscles refused to relax. They had finally stopped aching, but now they were as tense as if he had overpumped himself before a football game.

He rolled to the edge of the bed and stalked to the window. It was a strikingly different scene than what he had witnessed for the past few evenings, so peaceful and summerlike that he would easily have been able to think of those nights in the mountains as a strange fantasy. Of course, his fantasy would have included a beautiful woman and hours of wild, passionate sex. What he never would have considered including in that fantasy were the feelings of love and possessiveness that were now twisting his heart.

His chuckle was confused and devoid of any humor. For a man who liked the sex, but hated the even more intimate act of sleeping together, he was desperately lonely without Jamie in his arms and in his bed. He couldn't bear the thought of going to sleep without her or waking up alone. How ironic that he should feel that way about the one woman who would never agree to any sort of living arrangement other than the ultimate commitment.

He paced around the room, trying to list all the reasons he could never marry. But he kept coming back to the two most important ones—love and trust. Actually, they weren't two separate issues, but one that was intricately intertwined. Even if he let his guard down long enough to fall in love, he couldn't imagine ever being able to trust a woman. What would keep her from leaving him in the dark of the night? What would keep her from breaking his heart?

In spite of all the negatives, the thought of being with Jamie every day for the rest of their lives . . . or even as long as she decided to stay with him, was tempting. Maybe if they could talk about it, they could find a solution they could both accept.

Talk about it! Now that was a new twist. Matt had certainly never had a relationship with a woman in which conversation played an important part.

He pulled on his jeans, not bothering with the zipper and crossed to the door, unable to go another minute without seeing her. This could be the perfect moment to tell her he might be in love with her. Besides, he wanted to kiss her good-night and tuck her in.

Matt eased the door open and peeked into the hallway. The bathroom was directly across the wide hall and Jamie's room was beyond that. Never had such a short distance looked so far away.

He glanced around with the furtiveness of a thief, then straightened. He was a grown man and Jamie was a grown woman. If they wanted to entertain each other in their bedrooms, no one should think twice about it.

Matt stepped out and was heading toward her room when the bathroom door opened and Buck walked out.

"She's all yours, son," Buck said, idly scratching his balding head.

"She is?" Matt's jaw dropped.

"Sure, I'm through in there. I drank one glass of tea too many. The old bladder isn't what it used to be, you know."

Matt realized Buck was referring to the bathroom and not his daughter. "Oh yeah, sure. Same here," Matt said, changing direction and heading for the bathroom to keep Buck from suspecting his daughter was involved with Matt.

"I'm really sorry about not being able to lead the trail ride," Buck added as they passed each other. "I hope you weren't too disappointed."

"Oh, it wasn't too bad. I survived," Matt answered with what he hoped was a casual shrug. "Your daughter is an excellent guide."

"She probably knows these mountains as good as I do, and there ain't a horse she can't handle."

"You sound like you're pretty proud of her."

"Well, hell, of course I am. She works harder than any wrangler we have."

"I suppose you'll be sorry when she marries and moves away from the ranch."

"Jamie move away from the Rocky K? It'll never happen. She loves this ranch more than she could ever love a man. This land is everything to her. She'll never leave." He hiked up the waist of his pajama bottoms. "*If* she ever marries, and to be honest I don't think it's real likely, her husband would have to be willing to live here."

"Why don't you think she'll marry? She's a beautiful woman."

"I suppose she's not bad looking, even though she's not tiny like her mother was." He paused and a melancholy smile touched his lips. "But it would take a strong, patient man to be her husband. And, there ain't no one like that around here."

Matt knew it wasn't very charitable of him, but he was delighted to hear Buck's last statement.

"Boots tinkered with your car and got it running. But the radiator really needs to be replaced."

"I'll let the rental company worry about that," Matt said. "They're probably going to stick it to me, anyway, when I try to explain the accident. I doubt that covered wagons are considered an excusable road hazard."

"When do you suppose you'll be leaving? Not that we're trying to rush you off. You're welcome to stay as long as you want."

Matt gave him an appreciative smile. "Thanks for the offer, but I've got a book to write. I should have already been gone, but I'm going to stay for the rodeo tomorrow. I've never seen a real one before."

"Seen it! Hell, you're going to ride in it, aren't you?"

"I...uh...hadn't really considered it..."

"Of course you will. Everybody's looking forward to the competition. Don't take this wrong, but they all think it'd be an honor to outride the great Matt Montana."

"Then there should be a lot of very happy cowboys tomorrow," Matt muttered.

"What?"

"I said, then I won't disappoint all those happy cowboys," Matt said more loudly.

"Well, you'd better get some sleep so you'll be ready." Buck gave Matt an affectionate pat on the back, then headed past Jamie's door toward his own room at the opposite end of the hall.

That was all the confirmation Matt needed to know he had truly lost the last ounce of sense he'd ever had.

Buck stopped in his doorway and looked back at Matt, leaving the younger man no choice but to actually go into the bathroom.

JAMIE FINALLY gave up trying to sleep. She pulled a robe over the oversize Colorado Rockies baseball T-shirt she used as a gown and opened her bedroom door. Glancing first toward her father's room, she was pleased to see his door was shut.

She closed her door behind her and tiptoed across the hall to Matt's room. He might like to go down-stairs with her for a late-night snack...or maybe they'd think of a snack they could enjoy in his room.

His door was ajar and his light was off. Jamie peered into the darkness and saw a silhouette of his body on the bed. She watched for a few seconds, but when she didn't notice any movement, she sighed and took a step backward. How could he sleep? Had spending those nights with her meant so little that he didn't miss being with her at all?

"Looking for someone?"

She jumped straight into the air, startled by the whispered voice behind her ear. The unexpected up-ward movement of her shoulder caught Matt under the chin with a bone-jarring thud.

Matt muttered an oath and grabbed his chin and stumbled across the room until he collapsed on the edge of the bed.

"Oh, Matt, I'm sorry," Jamie said, following him to the bed. "Can I get you an icepack or a..."

His arms wrapped around her and pulled her onto the bed on top of him.

"Kiss it and make it better," he moaned, his breath tickling her face.

"Shh, you'll wake my father."

Matt slipped out of bed, tiptoed to the door and eased it shut. "He's already caught me roaming the halls once."

"Looking for someone?" she echoed, tilting her head playfully.

"Not anymore." He bounced across the room and pounced on her. The bed springs squeaked under them as they tumbled across the mattress, their arms and legs tangling in the sheets.

Her honey-gold hair splashed across his face as she lay on top of him. Her mouth was still parted in laughter as his fingers wrapped around the back of her head and pulled her closer until their lips met in a long, loving kiss.

Jamie's hands stroked his smooth cheeks. "You shaved your beard. I was beginning to get used to it. It felt so—" she paused, searching for the right word to describe the stimulation she had felt "—so sensual against my skin."

He pushed the robe off her shoulders and down her arms until it slid to the floor. "Let me show you how it feels without my beard," he murmured, his words soft and warm against her lips. "If you're not one hundred percent satisfied, I'll grow it back, just for you."

She knew that would be physically impossible since he was leaving Wednesday morning, which was less than thirty-six hours away. But it was nice to believe, for one more night, that he might stay right here in her arms forever.

"I've always been a sucker for money-back guarantees," she said, slipping her hands into his loosened jeans and stroking the warm skin of his buttocks. "What have I got to lose?" What did she have to lose indeed . . . he already had stolen her heart and spoiled her body so that she would never be satisfied by any other man.

The rest of their clothes were quickly discarded as they came together with the heat and passion of lovers long separated, rather than two people who had made love only the night before. Matt's clever hands found new erogenous areas on her body that she wasn't aware existed. His hungry lips covered her with kisses as he carried her to float among the stars in the summer sky before they fell asleep in each other's arms.

Sunlight streamed in the lacy curtains, and the sounds of a barnyard waking up crept into his open window. Matt picked out Maybelline's distinctive bray and the high-pitched crow of the orange and black bantam rooster that thought he was king of the roost. T-bone was barking at the back door, urging Darlene to hurry up with breakfast so he could dispose of the scraps. Funny how these same sounds that had set his teeth on edge now seemed so comforting.

Matt stretched and rolled over, gently so he wouldn't wake Jamie. He loved watching her sleep with her long dark eyelashes fanned across her surprisingly delicate cheekbones. Except for her large, expressive eyes and her full, rosy lips, all of her features were small and delightfully feminine, which seemed in direct contrast to her powerful, commanding personality. He would never have thought a woman who looked so sweet and beautiful could be so strong and efficient. But now that he'd seen what a dynamite combination it was, he would never settle for anything less.

He wanted to kiss her and tell her how much he loved waking up next to her each morning. He wanted to hold her sleep-softened body against his as they let the morning gradually ease into their senses until they were wide awake and ready to face another day together.

Together. It was a word Matt had never used in conjunction with himself and any other person. There hadn't been very many days of togetherness in his early life that revived happy memories. But he enjoyed spending every waking...and sleeping moment with Jamie. Together.

But Jamie was already gone. The pillow on her side of the bed was still indented with the shape of her head. Her scent still clung to the sheets that had been folded back as she got up.

Disappointment washed over him. He wasn't used to a woman getting out of his bed and leaving him. He was always the first to leave. Until that moment he'd never realized it was such a painful form of rejection, however unintentionally personal.

How long had she stayed with him? Had she merely awakened earlier than he and left quietly so as not to disturb him? Or had she sneaked back to her room in the middle of the night, ashamed of their relationship and unwilling to let anyone find out about it? Was this how he'd made the other women he'd known feel? Had he been that insensitive?

Matt sat on the edge of his bed and raked his fingers through his tangled hair. Yes, he was probably guilty of all those things. And now that he'd felt the sting of rejection, he was very sorry for his cavalier attitude. Being on the receiving end wasn't much fun.

THE LONG, CIRCULAR DRIVE and the guest parking area were all packed with cars and trucks, with more vehicles lining the county road for several hundred yards in both directions. Matt hadn't realized there were so many people living in the area. The Rocky K rodeo must be a bigger deal than he'd expected.

Terrific! That meant he would be humiliated in front of a lot more spectators than he'd anticipated.

But still, expecting to be thrown and possibly, considering his luck with horses, stomped into the earth, riding in the rodeo was something he had to do.

Boots loaned Matt some chaps, and Buck gave him a pair of antique Spanish spurs. Earlier that morning as Matt had dressed in his room, he'd felt like a bullfighter preparing to confront the biggest, meanest bull of his career.

There had been a knock on his door and Jamie had peered around the edge.

"Are you decent?" she'd asked.

"Is that a trick question?"

She had stepped inside and walked up to where he'd sat, pulling on his boots. "You don't have to ride in the rodeo. Don't let Buck bully you into it."

"Buck has nothing to do with me deciding to ride . . . or try to ride today."

Jamie gave him an exasperated look. "I thought you were getting over trying to prove how macho you are. You don't need to break your neck to impress me."

"It isn't because of you or your father or anyone else. And it isn't because I'm trying to prove my masculinity." Matt picked up one spur and twirled the silver rowel. "I don't know how to explain it, but I'm doing this for me, to prove something to myself. I exercise, I pretend I'm a tough guy, I talk a good game. But this is real. It's just the horse and me, testing what I've learned during the past week. I guess it's sort of like a final exam. I've been to school and now it's time to see if I could possibly have made it as a cowboy."

He could see from her expression that she didn't quite understand the difference between his masculine pride and his need to succeed at something she considered so trivial. Matt wasn't sure he understood it himself. He just knew he *had* to follow through. Whether or not he rode that horse until the horn sounded was not as important as the fact that he was willing to risk his reputation and his thirty-two year old bones to try.

"Okay, if you're determined to risk life and limb," Jamie added, shaking her head in disbelief, "then here's something for luck."

He looked up expectantly.

Jamie untied the bright red scarf she was wearing and stepped closer until she could loop it around his neck, then she leaned forward and kissed him. "You'll

be my Prince Charming, wearing my token into battle. Just remember, you have to keep one hand in the
air, but you can hang on tight to the saddlehorn with
your other hand. And if you get bucked off, try to be
relaxed when you hit the ground, but get out of the
way of the horse's hooves as quickly as possible. They
can do some real damage, considering they're sup-
porting a half ton of animal."

"Try not to sugarcoat it so much."

"I want you to know what you're getting into."

"What's another bruise or two?"

"I don't want you to hurt anything important." A
slow, suggestive smile lifted the corners of her mouth
and erased some of the concern in her eyes.

He was crazy about her dry sense of humor. But at
this particular moment, he wished she would be serious. He believed her when she'd finally admitted that
she'd had only one other lover, and Matt was glad she
enjoyed making love with him. However, he wanted to
know that she valued other things about their relationship. He didn't want her to think just about sex
whenever she was with him. It made him feel sort of
used, his other, more important qualities unappre-
ciated. It dawned on him that perhaps the women in
his books and even the women he'd known in the last
few years had felt the same way, and for the first time
he could feel genuine empathy with them.

And now as he walked toward the indoor riding
arena behind the mess hall, his adrenaline was pump-
ing. He couldn't remember the last time he was so
nervous. And yet he was also extremely excited by the
challenge. He was riding to bring his Western adven-

ture full circle. Soon it would be over and he would be back in his apartment, sitting in front of his computer and drawing from his experiences to add new energy to his books.

The chaps flapped against the outside of his legs as he walked, and the spurs clanged with every step. Matt felt like he'd stepped off a movie screen and expected Clint Eastwood to ride up at any minute.

Instead, it was T-bone who caught up to Matt and followed close on his heels as they joined the crowd milling around the booths where local 4-H and Scout groups were selling hot dogs and soft drinks.

Matt hadn't eaten since breakfast, but the butterflies in his stomach effectively filled the space. However, it was evident by T-Bone's pleading eyes that he had plenty of room for a hot dog or two.

"Okay, you moocher," Matt said, digging into his jeans pocket for his wallet. "Do you like your hot dogs with mustard or onions?"

T-bone barked three times.

Matt handed a dollar to the young girl behind the counter. "Two hot dogs, plain."

T-bone took the treats from Matt's hand with gentlemanly restraint, then gobbled them down. Matt rubbed the dog's spotted ears.

"Will all the riders please report behind the chutes," the announcer's voice boomed over the loudspeaker.

Matt gave T-bone one last pat and headed toward the end of the arena where the chutes were located.

Jamie explained the rules, for the benefit of those guests who were participating in the amateur events for the first time, and Buck drew the names of the horses for the riders from a cowboy hat. Matt was momentarily pleased his horse had the relatively calm name of Digger until he found out his full name was Gravedigger.

For whatever sadistic reason, Buck had scheduled Matt to ride last in the amateur saddle bronc division. Not only did Matt have to wait while the butterflies grew more violent, but he had to watch several painful-looking falls. There were a few bruised egos, but luckily, no one was seriously hurt. But then Matt hadn't had his chance to publicly humiliate himself yet.

When it was finally his turn, he pulled his black hat down tight on his forehead before climbing the rails of the bucking chute. Boots held Digger's head while Matt balanced over the saddle.

The roan gelding's eyes were rimmed in white as he glared backward at his would-be rider.

"Do you have a brother named Terminator?" Matt asked as he eased into the saddle.

The horse exhaled a blast of air through his flared nostrils.

"You ready?" Boots asked.

Matt wrapped the rope around his gloved hand like Buck had showed him, gripped the strap rigging across the pommel that replaced the large, dangerous saddlehorn, then gave a tight nod.

Digger exploded from the chute as soon as the gate swung open. Matt thought he was ready, but the burst of coiled energy surprised him, and several inches of daylight showed between his behind and the saddle seat. He landed back on the hard leather surface with a thud, and his knees automatically squeezed to steady himself. The horse bounded around the arena, stiff-legged, like four pogo sticks gone wild. Matt tried to spur the horse's shoulders, but Digger didn't need any encouragement to keep bucking.

Every time the horse's hooves hit the ground, it sent bone-jarring shock waves up through Matt's body. He clenched his jaw to keep his teeth from rattling as they made one lap of the arena.

It was the longest six seconds of his life. How the professional riders survived eight seconds was beyond belief. All Matt could think about was how glad he was that they'd cut the time for the amateurs. He felt as if he and Digger were moving in slow motion, with each second standing out clearly, stretching dangerously as the horse's determination to unseat his rider grew. Matt rose and fell with Digger's movements, equally determined to stick on that saddle like a tick on T-bone.

From somewhere in the distance the sound of an airhorn split the air, even louder than the cheering of the crowd. The ride was over. He'd made it.

But Digger didn't stop bucking. Matt gripped the straps with both hands. His time was out, but how could he get the message across to Digger?

Jamie galloped up, guiding Stormy as close to the bucking horse as she dared.

"How...do I...get off...?" Matt yelled between jolts.

Jamie reached over and unfastened Digger's bucking harness. The padded strap that pinched his flanks, causing him to buck fell to the ground. In theory, the horse should have calmed. But in reality, he continued to crowhop around the ring, bucking for the pure pleasure of it. Jamie called to Matt, "Grab hold of me and swing up behind my saddle."

"Easy...for you...to say." He unwrapped his hand from the strap, but continued clinging to the rigging until Jamie urged Stormy closer. Matt kicked his feet free of the stirrups and was about to leap when Digger gave a mighty kick, vaulting Matt into the air.

He caught Jamie's waist on the way down. She reached over and grabbed his belt, holding him up until he could swing his leg over her horse's rump. Triumphantly he settled behind her and waved to the crowd as they trotted out of the arena.

"I did it. I went the distance."

Jamie glanced over her shoulder and smiled. "I can't call you a dude anymore. You've earned your spurs."

"They'll come in real handy in Chicago."

He could feel her body tense, but her tone was light. "The next thing you know, you'll catch yourself listening to Garth Brooks songs and hanging out in country and western bars."

Matt chuckled and slid to the ground when Jamie stopped behind the chutes. "I'm not even sure if they have country and western bars in Chicago."

"How awful!" Jamie exclaimed with mock horror. "Poor Matt. No wonder you're the way you are."

"What's that supposed to mean?"

Jamie leaned over and surprised him with a kiss. "It means you've come a long way, baby." She pulled the reins to the side, and Stormy whirled around and galloped back toward the arena so Jamie could assist the riders in the professional division.

"What does *that* mean?" Matt asked again. He had a sneaking suspicion she wasn't referring to his improved riding skills.

THERE WAS ANOTHER dance after the rodeo. A hardwood floor had been laid out on top of the arena's dirt floor, and what seemed to be a couple hundred people circled to the music. The hometown country band was fine-tuning their skills for the annual bluegrass festival that would be held in the nearby town of Telluride the following weekend.

Matt joined in, dancing with many different partners, celebrating his amateur win. A ridiculously large silver-plated belt buckle shone even in the dimmed lights, drawing the women as if it were some sort of magnet. But all the while, as he accepted compliments on his books and his riding prowess and flirted outrageously but harmlessly, he kept his eyes focused on Jamie.

She, too, wasn't lacking for partners, but she kept glancing in his direction. When the band finally played a slow-paced love song, Matt excused himself from his current partner and crossed the dance floor until he stood next to Jamie and the man with whom she had been dancing.

"I believe she promised this dance to me," Matt said. The other man looked at Jamie, and when she nodded, he stepped away and Matt took his place.

They exchanged a long, wistful glance, then Jamie moved closer and rested her head on his shoulder as he tucked her hand against his chest. Their steps slowed as their bodies swayed to a private internal rhythm of their own.

As always when he held her, desire burned within him. But this time, there was something more. They both knew this might be the last time they would ever be in each other's arms. Matt's glare discouraged any man who approached, intent on cutting in. He was determined to make the moment stretch as long as possible.

When the song ended, they were near the chutes. Without discussion, they walked, hand in hand, behind the chutes and outside to the corral where the bucking stock was milling around.

Matt braced his back against the fence rails and Jamie stood between his legs, her body pressed to his.

"I'm leaving in the morning," he whispered, rubbing his cheek against the top of her head as she leaned against his chest.

"I know." There was a moment's silence, then she added in a voice so soft, he had to strain to hear it, "Do you think you'll ever be back in this area?"

"I can't make any promises."

There was another long pause before Jamie leaned back and looked him directly in the eyes. "I can't imagine why your mother left when you were so young. But you shouldn't judge all women by that. Most are able to make lasting commitments."

"It takes lots of trust."

"And love."

He studied her eyes, searching for an answer to a question he dared not ask. But she was hesitant, holding back until he made the first move . . . a move he couldn't make.

"Will I see you later tonight?" he asked.

She was fighting back the tears as she shook her head. "No, you'll need the time to pack. I think it's better if we say our goodbyes now."

"I wish we had more time to talk this through. But I have to get back and finish that book."

"And I have to stay here and take care of the ranch and my father."

Matt heaved a frustrated sigh. "Jamie, I don't want it to end like this."

"You're the author. Write us a different ending."

"It's the only ending I know."

"Whatever happened to riding off into the sunset together?"

"That only happens in fiction and bad movies."

Her fingers trailed down the square ridge of his jaw in a tender caress. "I believe in happy endings," she cried, then pivoted and ran toward the house.

He wanted to run after her, but he forced himself to stay. However, wild horses couldn't have kept him from watching her until she disappeared into the night and aching more with each step that separated them. "I wish I could, too," he whispered.

JAMIE DIDN'T KNOW how she survived the next month. Guests arrived and left as scheduled. She resumed her duties with the wagon train while her father, who had made a miraculous recovery, led the trail rides, all without further incident.

She met the mailman every day. There was a letter from Dale reassuring her that he was recovering nicely and didn't hold her or the Rocky K responsible for his accident. There were more reservations, especially after an article appeared in *People* magazine about Matt's stay at the ranch and how it inspired his latest book, *Once a Desperado*. The storyline was top secret, but his publisher was already planning a massive publicity tour for its release next year.

But the letter she never got and wanted most was from Matt. She understood why he left. They'd both been confused and hesitant to take the next step. And they both had responsibilities that pulled them in different directions.

However, she'd fully expected to hear from him again. But as the days passed with no letter or phone call, she began to face the painful truth that once he'd gotten back home, his old life had taken over. Other women filled his thoughts and his arms. Jamie had obviously meant nothing to him. He was no different from that jerk from Atlanta.

But deep in her heart, she couldn't believe that. Matt had never actually told her he loved her...not in so many words. Words were his life, and yet he had major difficulty voicing his feelings.

Jamie wished she'd told him how she felt. Maybe if she'd admitted that she loved him, it might have broken up all those emotions he'd kept in check for so many years. And now she would never have the opportunity.

She knew, instinctively, that she would never love that way again. Eventually she might meet someone

else who could make her laugh and satisfy her in bed.
And she might even be able to fall in love again. But
it would never be as intense or as filled with breathless wonder as her love for Matt.

Maybe it was impossible for that kind of love to last.
Perhaps it flared hot and bright for a short while, then
burned itself out. By leaving, Matt hadn't given it time
to run its course.

Jamie sat on the top rail of the corral and watched
the latest set of dudes bounce around on their horses'
backs as they got acquainted with their mounts. She
couldn't help remembering the first day Matt had ridden Terminator. In fact, there wasn't anything that
happened around the ranch that didn't revive a memory about Matt.

Oh, how she missed him. She sighed and pressed her
hand against her chest, trying to ease the ache cen-
tered there. She wasn't eating, she wasn't sleeping, she
was distracted from the guests. She wished she could
see Matt just once more to test the theory that absence made the heart grow fonder. Now that she
hadn't seen him in more than a month, would her
heart still skitter erratically whenever he so much as
looked at her, and would her breath still catch in her
throat as she watched him sleep?

She had no doubt his touch would ignite those feminine fires deep inside her, but it was more than that.
She loved making love with him, but she also loved
sitting by the lake watching his delight when a fish finally took his bait and his dismay at having to take it
off the hook. She loved the shape and texture of his

magnificent body, but she also loved the intelligence
that sparkled in his eyes and challenged her own wits.

The last night on the trail they'd taken their sleeping bags outside and lay in the middle of a meadow,
staring up at countless stars that glittered overhead.
He'd pointed out the constellations, even though he'd
never actually seen them in his city sky. It was one
more thing he'd learned from books, but discovered
during his vacation.

Jamie looked around her at the majestic silhouette
of the Rockies against the hot, blue summer sky. This
had to be the most beautiful place on earth. How
could he leave it? How could he leave her? How could
she live the rest of her life without him?

She had to know. She had to talk to him, face-to-
face, one more time to see if it was real. Had she been
caught up in his "Western adventure" or had she met
that one man with whom she would live happily ever
after? Was she willing to make major changes in her
life-style to adapt to his?

She let her gaze caress the green of the trees and the
serenity of the horses and cattle grazing in the pas-
tures. Could she give all this up for the love of Matt?

Her eyelids drifted closed, and she saw him looking
back at her with that sexy grin lifting the corners of his
lips and his deep blue eyes shining with what had appeared to be genuine affection.

She had to know. She simply couldn't go through
the rest of her life wondering if she'd ever hear from
him again, waiting for him to return, not knowing if
she'd been a passing fling or if they might have had a
chance at something wonderful.

The sound of a horse approaching her caused her to open her eyes. With the sun behind him, the man's broad shoulders could have been Matt's. So could the long, jean-covered legs and the black cowboy hat that rested at a jaunty angle on the man's head. Even the way he sat on the saddle, a little too loose, and held the reins a little too tight looked very much the way Matt had ridden.

"Hi," the man said in a voice that was definitely not Matt's. "Your name's Jamie, isn't it?"

Trying to mask her extreme disappointment, Jamie nodded. "Yes, and you're Eric, right?"

He rode close enough so she could clearly see his face. It was every bit as handsome as Matt's, and he was every bit as cocky. But he had none of Matt's charisma or powerful personality... at least as far as Jamie was concerned.

"Right." He flashed her a wide, flirtatious smile, apparently unaware that she was totally oblivious to his charm, charm that had, no doubt, worked on many women before her. "So what do you do for fun around here?"

Jamie returned his smile, although her sudden cheer had nothing to do with the man next to her. "Go to Chicago," she announced, hopping down from the fence.

Eric looked confused. "That's a little extreme, isn't it?"

But Jamie was already striding across the corral to where her father was instructing the beginners.

"I'm leaving, Dad," she announced.

"Going into town? Pick me up some shaving cream. I ran out..."

"I don't know when I'll be back."

"That's okay. I don't need it until tomorrow morning."

"No, I mean I might not be coming back...ever," she said. "Or I might be back in a couple of days. It pretty much depends on the weather in Chicago."

"What?"

"If it's hot, I'll stay. If it's cool I'll be on the next plane home."

Buck looked blank for a few seconds, then nodded wisely. "Does Matt know you're coming?"

"No, I want to be able to read his genuine reaction. And don't you dare call and warn him."

"Of course I wouldn't." Buck's expression suddenly changed to one of near panic. "But you can't leave. What about the guests? What about the ranch?"

"You can handle it."

"No, I can't. I need you." He waved his hand around in a large circle. "We all need you. This ranch has never run so smoothly. If it wasn't for you, I'd have been forced to sell by now."

Jamie was shocked. She'd never heard her father give her any credit for anything, much less saving the ranch. But the ranch was no longer her only love.

"I'll call you and let you know." She took his gloved hands in hers and looked into his weather-worn face. "But I've got to go see Matt."

"I was hoping you two hardheaded mavericks would fall in love. But," Buck growled, "this isn't working out right. I wanted to add a son-in-law, not lose my daughter.''

"You planned this?''

"Well, not all of it. I had nothing to do with him coming to the ranch originally. But once God dropped him into our laps, I thought I'd try to make the best of it.''

"Your back was fine, wasn't it?''

Buck grimaced. "It had felt better.''

Jamie gave him a stern stare, then softened it with a kiss to his leathery cheek. "I never realized you were a frustrated matchmaker.''

"And I never considered the possibility that you'd leave the ranch for good.'' He shuffled his feet. "Maybe I haven't always told you, but I'm gosh darn proud of you, girl.''

"Thanks, Dad.'' Jamie's eyes filled with tears. "You don't know how much it means to me for you to say that.'' She knew how easily displays of emotion embarrassed Buck, but she couldn't resist a quick hug.

"Now get along, girl,'' Buck muttered, his eyes unusually bright. "I hope he makes you happy.''

"I don't know what to hope. I just want to talk to him again.'' Among other things, she didn't add out loud.

She rushed to make flight reservations and pack a bag. She had only an hour to make her flight, and it was a good forty-minute drive to the airport, so she would have to hustle. After tossing her suitcase and overnight bag on the seat of her small, four-wheel-drive pickup truck, she backed out of the carport and headed down the driveway, then turned onto the county road. The crushed rock spun out behind her wheels as she pushed down on the accelerator.

Now that her decision had been made and her plan put into action, Jamie was anxious to be in Chicago. She had written down Matt's address and telephone number and would take a taxi to his apartment. She had no concrete ideas of what she would do next. Hopefully, Matt would be glad to see her, and they would be able to sit down and talk.

Oh Lord, what if he wasn't alone? What if there was a woman cooking his dinner or warming his bed? What if he had plans for the evening and left her standing on his doorstep?

Well, that, in itself, would be an answer. Then she could come back to Colorado and get on with her life.

A woman in his kitchen! A woman in his bed! Those thoughts were not so easily dismissed. Of course, he'd dated other women. But that was *before* he met Jamie.

Distracted by the image of Matt's naked body lying next to a beautiful redhead caused Jamie to take the curve a little faster than she should have. The truck swung wide, its tires gripping the road, but the loose gravel caused the rear end to fishtail wildly.

She didn't see the horse until it was too late. Luckily, the horse saw her and made a split-second defensive maneuver that took him out of the line of the speeding truck. Unfortunately, the horse's rider didn't react as quickly.

He left the saddle, rocketing through the air until he landed, with a thud and a groan, on the hood of her truck. Jamie slammed on the brakes and her momentum kept the guy plastered to the windshield until the truck jolted to a stop on the grassy shoulder of the road. The sudden change of motion sent the man sliding down the hood and tumbling to the ground.

Jamie turned off the engine, threw the gears into park and leapt out of the truck. "Are you hurt? I didn't see you..."

He was dressed all in white, white jeans, white long-sleeved shirt, white cowboy hat. Only his boots were gray: scuffed gray ostrich-skin boots. "Matt?" She rolled him over, and the hat fell off his dark brown hair. His eyes were shut, his thick, black lashes lying much too still on his cheeks.

"Oh, God, Matt, don't you dare die." She grabbed the front of his shirt and shook him, then collapsed on his chest, sobbing. "You idiot. You're supposed to be in Chicago with some slut cooking your dinner. Open your eyes, dammit. I'm not going to lose you now. I love you. Oh, Matt, I love you so much."

"It's about time you told me that."

Jamie sat up and was delighted to see his brilliant blue eyes staring back at her.

"I want to hear it again," he said.

"Hear what?"

"That you love me." He frowned. "I can't quite figure out the part about the slut cooking my dinner."

"Never mind. But you better not have zipped up any sleeping bags since you left."

"I think you must have hit *your* head."

"I missed you, you jerk."

"Not really," he commented wryly with an eloquent glance at his position on the ground. He wrapped his arms around her and pulled her back down on top of him. "I was going to surprise you."

"Well, you did that." She looked around at the white horse calmly grazing by the roadside. "Where'd you get the horse?"

"Hertz Rent-a-Horse," he joked. "You know it's more difficult to rent a horse than it is a car?"

"That's because your driving record preceded you."

He glanced up at her truck. "Look who's talking."

"I was in a hurry. I wanted to see you again and find out how you felt about our relationship."

"Would a guy dress up like this and come charging down the road on a white horse if he wasn't wildly, insanely...with the emphasis on insanely...in love?"

Jamie's heart was skittering, and her breath was catching in her throat even more than the last time she'd looked into his dear face. "In love?"

He nodded. "I can't think of any other reason for why I've felt so lousy since I got back to Chicago."

"Why didn't you write...or call?"

"Because I was determined to prove that I didn't love you and didn't need you."

"And?"

"I missed you like hell. All I proved was that I *do* love you and I *do* need you." His gorgeous grin stretched across his gorgeous face. "The good news is I wrote my book in a month. And my editor loves it."

"Duke King..."

"Dude. No, it's *Duke*." Matt rolled his eyes. "Now you've got me saying it."

"The one and only *Duke* vanquishes another band of outlaws and saves a town while making love with the local schoolmarm?"

"It started out that way," Matt admitted. "But somewhere along the way, the schoolmarm captured his heart."

"Duke King fell in love!" Jamie chuckled.

"Yeah, can you believe it? Me and Duke, the last two desperadoes taken out by women."

Matt cradled her face between his big hands and tenderly kissed her. "Hmm, I've missed that. I think I might have some boo-boos that need your attention. And I have a feeling this is a trend for the future. You're a dangerous woman, Jamie Kimball." He kissed her again, a long, lingering kiss that left them both breathless. "And I love you more than I've ever loved anyone or anything in my life."

"Does this mean you're going to stick around here for a while?"

"Forever if you'll have me. I finally got these damn boots broken in, and they just didn't fit in with Chicago chic."

"How sweet," Jamie drawled wryly. "You've come back because your feet stopped hurting."

The vibrations of his chuckle rippled through her body. "Maybe my feet don't hurt anymore, but there are other parts of my body that have been aching for you since the first moment we met." He wiggled his eyebrows suggestively.

An ancient, rust-corroded pickup truck pulled to a stop and a rancher jumped out. "Has there been an accident? Are y'all hurt?"

Matt stood, pulling Jamie up with him. "No, sir, we were just having a discussion."

"In the middle of the dang road? You could get killed."

Matt walked to the horse and vaulted into the saddle, a little shakily, but with great style. He held out his arm and said, "Come on, Jamie. Boots can come back for the truck. Let's go talk to your pa. It's about time I made an honest woman of you."

Jamie put her foot in the stirrup, grabbed his hand and let him pull her up in front of him.

"And we need to find ourselves a preacher," Matt declared, nuzzling his face into the softness of her hair. "This story's going to have a happy ending."

Epilogue

He'd faced crazed killers, angry rattlesnakes and grumpy grizzlies. But never, in his entire life, had he been so downright scared.

Duke paced the floor, wishing he knew what to do next. He'd always prided himself on his nerves of steel, but here he was, reduced to a blithering idiot. How had he let himself get caught in this situation? He was a man who never let grass grow under his boots. He was a man who lived by his wits, not his emotions.

And yet, faced with this most terrifying experience, his logic deserted him. He was as helpless as a newborn puppy or a . . .

The baby's cry split the air. It was loud and shrill with anger, and it was the best sound Duke had ever heard.

"It's a girl," the doctor declared, carrying a wet, screaming infant out of the bedroom. "You've got yourself a mighty healthy daughter, Duke."

Duke looked into the wrinkled, red face and felt a love and protectiveness so fierce it was like a physical pain. His daughter. Duke King was a father. Any question that he might be disappointed that it was not *a son was dispelled when the tiny fingers wrapped around his in a surprisingly strong grasp.*

"How's Rebecca? Can I see her?" he asked the doctor.

"She's fine. Go right on in. I'm sure she'll be glad to have you with her."

There was a knock on the door and the sheriff burst in. "There's a whole gang of—

"Matt, could you hold Becky for a minute? I've got to run out to the barn and check on Stormy. She should be foaling any minute now."

Matt turned away from the computer screen and took his beautiful baby daughter into his arms.

"Here's her bottle. Bobby's still asleep, but his bottle's ready if he wakes up. I'll be back as soon as possible."

"No hurry. I can handle the babies."

Jamie gave him a skeptical smile. "The last time I left you alone with the twins, you went to bed early with a headache."

"Yes, but the twins were fed and dry and sound asleep when you got back." Ever since they'd found that preacher six years ago, Matt had been absolutely honest with Jamie. It was useless to put on an act with her, anyway, because she could read him like a book— so to speak. But he would never admit how hard he'd had to work that first time she'd left him alone with the twins. They'd kept him running, feeding, changing, rocking and trying to get them both to sleep at the same time.

But he'd developed a system now. He'd even learned how to type with one hand while holding a baby in the other arm.

Jamie dropped a kiss on Becky's soft, fuzzy head, then paused for a much longer kiss on Matt's lips. "Darlene's offered to baby-sit for us tonight if Stormy has her foal, maybe we could drive into Telluride for dinner and a movie."

He ran his free hand up her leg until he cupped her firm rear. "Or we could park the car in the garage, turn off all the lights and work on a brother or sister for Becky and Bobby."

An ever-present spark of desire lit up her blue eyes. She leaned against him, intentionally rubbing the curve of her breast against his shoulder. "I'll hurry," she repeated, but this time it had a whole different meaning.

Matt turned back to his computer. He had only a few more pages before he finished his latest Duke King adventure. He was going to have trouble getting Duke out of his wife's bedroom and in the street fighting the bad guys. Matt knew how fatherhood had mellowed him, and he had a feeling Duke would be similarly affected. But his fans seemed to love this new side of his literary hero. Sales even showed that more women were reading his Desperado series now.

Matt had never been happier, and the man Jamie had once accused of being his alter ego was happier now, too. No longer a desperado except by reputation, Duke, like Matt, chose to keep his woman by his side. It created another whole level of conflict to the stories, but it also added an element that made Jamie extremely happy... Duke and his wife, Rebecca were always riding off into the sunset together, on their way to a new adventure.

Matt and Jamie's firm family ties kept them closer to home, helping Buck run the ranch while Matt produced more books in the Desperado series, and he and Jamie raised their children in the New West. But almost every evening when the weather cooperated, he and Jamie sat on the rocks that surrounded their lake and watched the sun paint the sky with vivid colors as it sank into its rocky bed. They'd ridden all over the Rocky K, finally selecting this site for their house, because the lake reminded them both of that alpine lake where they'd really gotten to know each other.

The nipple fell out of Becky's mouth and she dozed peacefully in his arms, her lips still shaped in a tiny O. He knew he could take her to her bed now and she would sleep for several hours. But Matt had made a startling discovery on the day his kids were born.

He was a good father. And it was a role he loved, almost as much as he loved being Jamie's husband. His own unhappy childhood had faded far in the past, replaced by the excitement and pleasure of his new family. When once he'd thought himself incapable of love, he now felt so much love it filled every pore of his body.

Matt pressed the Save button on his computer, then turned it off. He could finish Duke's story later. Right now he wanted to sit on the back porch and hold his daughter in his arms. He was busy making memories that would last a lifetime.

HE HAD TO BE REAL

Did ghosts have silky hair and piercing eyes? Were their bodies lean and hard? Emily Morrell didn't think so. But Captain Calvert T. Witherspoon, late of His Majesty's service, *was* walking through walls. Emily heard the rumors about Henderson House being haunted, but she didn't know her intoxicating fantasy ghost was more man than she could handle.

CHARLOTTE MACLAY brings you a delightful tale next month, about a ghost with a very special touch . . .

#488 A GHOSTLY AFFAIR
by Charlotte Maclay
May 1993

When a man loves a woman, there's nothing he wouldn't do for her. . . .

For a close encounter of the most sensual kind, don't miss American Romance #488 A GHOSTLY AFFAIR.

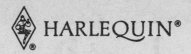 **HARLEQUIN®**

THE TAGGARTS OF TEXAS!

Harlequin's Ruth Jean Dale brings you
THE TAGGARTS OF TEXAS!

Those Taggart men—strong, sexy and hard to resist...

You've met Jesse James Taggart in FIREWORKS!
Harlequin Romance #3205 (July 1992)

And Trey Smith—he's THE RED-BLOODED YANKEE!
Harlequin Temptation #413 (October 1992)

And the unforgettable Daniel Boone Taggart in SHOWDOWN!
Harlequin Romance #3242 (January 1993)

Now meet Boone Smith and the Taggarts who started it all—
in LEGEND!
Harlequin Historical #168 (April 1993)

Read all the Taggart romances!
Meet all the Taggart men!

Available wherever Harlequin Books are sold.

HARLEQUIN PRESENTS®

A Year
DOWN UNDER

In 1993, Harlequin Presents celebrates the land down
under. In May, let us take you to Auckland, New Zealand,
in SECRET ADMIRER by Susan Napier,
Harlequin Presents #1554.

Scott Gregory is ready to make his move. He's realized
Grace is a novice at business *and* emotionally vulnerable—
a young widow struggling to save her late husband's
company. But Grace is a fighter. She's taking business
courses and she's determined not to forget Scott's
reputation as a womanizer. Even if it means adding
another battle to the war—a fight against her growing
attraction to the handsome New Zealander!

Share the adventure—and the romance—
of A Year Down Under!

Available this month in
A YEAR DOWN UNDER

A DANGEROUS LOVER
by Lindsay Armstrong
Harlequin Presents #1546
Wherever Harlequin books are sold.

YDU-A

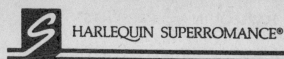

HARLEQUIN SUPERROMANCE®

HARLEQUIN SUPERROMANCE NOVELS WANTS TO INTRODUCE YOU TO A DARING NEW CONCEPT IN ROMANCE . . .

WOMEN WHO DARE!
Bright, bold, beautiful . . .
Brave and caring, strong and passionate . . .
They're women who know their own minds
and will dare anything . . .
for love!

One title per month in 1993, written by popular Superromance authors, will highlight our special heroines as they face unusual, challenging and sometimes dangerous situations.

Next month, time and love collide in:
#549 PARADOX by Lynn Erickson
Available in May wherever Harlequin Superromance novels are sold.